Leonardo Forever

For Carol, with much love.

Omnibus Books
An imprint of Scholastic Australia Pty Limited
(ABN 11 000 614 577)
PO Box 579 Gosford NSW 2250
www.scholastic.com.au

Part of the Scholastic Group
Sydney • Auckland • New York • Toronto • London • Mexico City
New Delhi • Hong Kong • Buenos Aires • Puerto Rico

Published by Omnibus Books in 2023.

Cover and internals designed by Grace Felstead.

A catalogue record for this book is available from the National Library of Australia

ISBN: 978-1-76120-326-8

Typeset in Adobe Garamond Pro and Aphrodite Slim Text.

Printed by McPherson's Printing Group, Maryborough, VIC.

Scholastic Australia's policy, in association with McPherson's Printing Group, is to use papers that are renewable and made efficiently with wood from responsibly managed sources, so as to minimise its environmental footprint.

The paper in this book is FSC® certified.
FSC® promotes environmentally responsible, socially beneficial and economically viable management of the world's forests.

23 24 25 26 27 / 2

Leonardo Forever

Richard Yaxley

Every age is fed on illusions.

—Joseph Conrad

Contents

Prologue

September 1466: Florence, Italy.
The bottega of Andrea del Verrocchio, master artist.

When they reached the studio, his father strode inside but the boy was slower, preferring to stop near the entrance where the light was strong enough for him to observe a multitude of wonders. The master had left sketches out, some fanned across the floor, others laying on a table or propped on easels. One easel was broader and higher than the rest and the boy stood directly in front of it to see the focus of Verrocchio's next project: the Madonna, looking tired but serene beneath what would no doubt become a shimmering, golden halo. He blinked at the beauty before him, then moved closer so as to properly absorb the elegance of the composition: the lightness of the headdress with its bow and tassels, and the graceful flutes and folds in the Madonna's gown. The tenderness with which the Madonna's hands cradled the Saviour was already majestic, as was the rendering of the child's halo, poised above a crown of russet curls.

Delicate curls, noted the boy, as well as trusting eyes and arms outstretched in an obvious call for love. He looked more closely at the child's face and was startled by the resemblance to his friend, his dear friend—but was that resemblance real or in his mind only? Was this artist's impression yet another reminder that only God's work is truth, and humans can do no more than create copies of that work, copies which will inevitably be inferior?

He looked away, blinked, looked back. Oh, the enchantment of those eyes!

'Leo!' His father tapped his shoulder. 'Enough daydreaming. Verrocchio is not a man to be kept waiting.'

The boy offered an apologetic murmur and followed his father into the *bottega*, past drying panels, benches, kilns and pottery wheels. A number of the apprentices called greetings.

'Good morning, Piero! Is this your clever son?'

'He is far prettier than you! Look at those luscious locks!'

'Where is *your* hair, old notary?'

Ser Piero da Vinci laughed good-naturedly along with them. He was holding a roll of scuff-edged papers, which he now brandished as if it were a weapon.

'You will see! Talentless fools!'

They walked through the bustle to the side of the studio. Here, where the light streamed through high windows, a man was supervising three nervous young painters.

'A *gentle* grip!' he said. 'Gentle!' He waggled his large head in exasperation and pointed to the middle panel. 'Saverio, I despair! You paint like a bull.'

'In a field full of cows,' added one of the other young men, receiving a cuff on the back of his head and a curse for his trouble.

'Andrea?'

'Ah, Piero.' The man lowered his pointer, issued a brief instruction and left his students.

Leo saw that the master, though still young, was already round-faced, with the ruddy complexion of someone who ate well and frequently. The two men embraced, then stood awkwardly until Verrocchio gestured towards the painters.

'More devotionals,' he said. 'Of course, I would rather have my apprentices perform simpler tasks, however we simply cannot keep up with the demand. Once, it was only the major guildsmen who charged in and rattled their *florins* expectantly. Now, every merchant in Florence wants a framed Madonna on his wall.'

'That is the fashion—'

'And I am a slave to that fashion. Well, it's a busy life and we all crave money.'

'We do—'

'Which is why I continue to say to my customers: yes, owning a Madonna is good, but owning a *Verrocchio*

Madonna is better. As it will be, if these dolts ever manage to produce anything that is worth selling.'

Piero smiled.

The men were quiet for a moment until Piero said, more formally, 'Andrea, I ask only that you view my son's work. After that—'

'I hear promising reports, and not all from you.' Verrocchio beckoned.

Piero untied the roll of papers and passed them over.

'We have been good friends for a number of years now.'

'Yes, we have. You have given me excellent service, Piero, and saved me much expense. I certainly appreciate that, however let us be clear. For your son to join my studio, he must, of course, have talent. But that alone is not enough. There are a thousand talented artists in this madhouse city and no doubt ten thousand more throughout Italy.' He scowled. 'Except, of course, in that cesspit Milan,' he said.

'That is true.'

Verrocchio touched Leo's face with the papers, a light caress.

'You are a handsome boy,' he said with an encouraging smile, 'and therefore nothing like your father. Be grateful for that.'

Piero laughed politely.

'However,' said the master, 'you are here as an aspiring artist, and all artists, regardless of their capacity, need to know what I am about to say. Leonardo, skill comes second to perseverance, and both are outranked by humility. An artist must be determined enough to succeed and humble enough to understand that his success, once achieved, will be fleeting and probably gained through the exertions of many, not just himself. Moreover, that success will in all likelihood lead to his continuing moral downfall, whether or not he wishes for that to happen.' He looked around at the activity within the *bottega*: the drawing and shaping, the banging and firing, the arguing. 'We all seek posterity,' he said, more seriously, 'but that special place is reserved for a very small number. Most of us are mere artisans, churning out works for those who are truly rich and those who delude themselves into presuming the same status. While our customers don their fancy silks and prance about the *piazzas*, we must work like dogs and hope for nothing more than to fill our tables with bread.'

'Or wine,' said Piero, smirking.

'That too. Well, boy? Are you determined? Are you humble?'

Leo bowed. 'I will learn,' he said. 'That is all I want.'

'Very good. Let us see what you can already do.'

Verrocchio unfurled the papers. On the top page he saw an old man's exquisitely ugly face in profile. The cross-hatchings were unusual, moving as they did on a downward slant from right to left, but the proportions and detail in the sketch were remarkable. The master's eyes widened as he began to work his way through the pages. He saw a flowing river edged by a perfect strata of rock. A dragon with minutely rendered scales and eyes that seemed to follow him, no matter the angle of viewing. A mechanical contraption with each pulley, rope and panel drawn finely and accurately. A wave and a leaf, both created in cross-section. Masquerade figures with elaborate helmets and doublets. An inquisitive ermine foraging for insects. The spiralling of a rose in bloom. A dove rising into flight. The front legs of a horse caught mid-gallop. And on one page, centred, a pair of lips drawn into a beguiling smile.

'Well? What do you think, old friend? Is my son ready to study with the great Andrea del Verrocchio?'

The master straightened. Leo noticed that the man's hands were shaking.

'Come with me,' he said.

CHAPTER 1

Arrival

April 1465: Vinci, Italy

Annalisa de Torriano sat glumly in the family carriage and replayed, in her mind, her father's most recent words.

'I have important business with the guild. You will go with your mother, Vanni and Luca to the *contado*.'

To the countryside! Her friend, Cosetta, visiting at the time, had told her what to expect from the drab north: flat, uninspiring hills, the river turned narrow and filthy, and those awful, muddy fields where the sharecroppers bent their thin bodies into coaxing wheat or beans from the silt. Not to mention the colourless sky and stinking meadows. Stinking everything!

Dismayed, she had stared at her father.

'To our new estate, child,' he had said proudly.

As an increasingly influential seller of spices, Alessandro de Torriano was now a member of the sixth major guild, giving him the opportunity to make new, valuable connections within the fabled rooms of the

Palazzo Vecchio. Guildsmen from this upper tier either had wealth or were well into the process of gaining wealth. Owning an estate in the country was highly desirable. Going to that estate for at least part of the summer was seen as both a reward for hard work and an attractive way of signalling the family's success within Florentine society.

But now? she thought. When her life was only just beginning . . .

The carriage jiggled and bumped. Already the road was unbearably rough, unlike the paved streets closer to home. Annalisa gritted her teeth and dared to look outside. They were on the edge of the city, far less appealing than the energetic, golden hub and unlikely to improve as their journey continued. The stunted, sour-looking people milling aimlessly around their hovels appalled her. The stench of mud and feral animals appalled her, as did the sounds of swearing workers and braying donkeys. Annalisa had hoped that Cosetta, who was always mindful of the advancement of self at the expense of others, may have been offering a biased view of the countryside. Her family preferred—and could afford—to spend their summers in a villa southwest of Florence, near the coast, rather than in the less fashionable area around the village of Vinci. However, it did not look like Cosetta had been exaggerating.

Annalisa pouted and thought how typical this was of her father, to promise a flower and unveil a weed.

Their exchange had continued. Annalisa, loved for being the sole daughter and several years younger than her brothers, had said, 'But, Father, what of my engagements?' When he hadn't answered, she'd offered her biggest, brightest smile and said, 'I have my music lessons. Maestro tells me that my finger work is improving.' Then she'd curtsied, stepped back and forth, and said, 'And I have my dancing. We are learning the *Galliard* and the *Tourdion* as alternatives to the *Bassadanza*. Father, the boring *Bassadanza!*'

That impassive face, those immovable eyes. Finally, he'd coughed and turned to the door.

'Martina will pack your clothes,' he'd said on his way out. 'Go, instruct her.'

They'd left after breakfast. Luca had laughed at her sad face.

'Vanni, look. Your sister is pretending again.'

'*My* sister?' grinned Vanni, the eldest.

'She must be yours. Such a talented tragedian couldn't possibly be related to me.'

'Is she a tragedian or a comedian? The line is narrow.'

'It is,' agreed Luca. 'Perhaps, in time, she will become a comic tragedian—'

'Or a tragic comedian!'

'Whichever best suits at the time. Either way, our Anna

is bound to join a troupe of players.'

'Oh, yes. She's a regular entertainer! She'll play the great halls of Europe—'

'The great paddocks of Puglia!'

'Don't tease,' their mother had admonished, her own eyes dancing with merriment.

Annalisa had ignored them all. Her family was infuriating!

Bump and jiggle. Bump and sway.

She closed her eyes and thought of her home on Via Palazzuolo, then of Florence itself. Could there be a happier, more stimulating place on Earth? Surely not! Florence was the New Rome, the centre of everything! The people were beautiful. Everyone wore the finest clothes sewn with thread made from copper or gold, and they spoke with great clarity and confidence about important matters that she hoped to one day understand. The River Arno was clean and wide and fragrant. The buildings, especially the Cathedral of Santa Maria del Fiore where she was sent to pray, were magnificent. There were games—Luca had been teaching her backgammon—and music, and the Medici family were generous in providing festivals and pageants. As well as all that, Annalisa had recently sat for her first individual portrait after her father had commissioned a promising local artist to produce the work. The prospect of seeing her portrait had excited her greatly—more proof that, in Florence, life was always worthwhile and memorable.

Yet here they were, heading for the *contado*!

There was another reason that Annalisa had been reluctant to leave Florence, one that she could not yet admit to her parents. His name was Matteo Piombino.

He was the eldest son of a wealthy silk merchant; their fathers had met occasionally in the guildhall. Annalisa had first seen Matteo at the marketplace. She'd had her furtive glances returned, then had met him properly at a festival where, while pretending to watch the jousting, they'd managed to touch fingertips. Matteo had the smooth, luxurious hair and well-oiled skin of an established Florentine lineage, as well as a shapely mouth, one that Annalisa had soon decided would be filled with lovely, loving promises. He was being groomed to join the banking business, but secretly wanted to go to university and study Greek.

'Theirs was the greatest civilisation in the history of the world,' he had told Annalisa during some precious, stolen moments beneath a bridge. 'I must know all there is to know about it.' He'd pushed out his scrawny chest and said grandly, 'I will join the Platonic Academy and everyone, including the Medicis, will be in awe of my knowledge.'

Such a joy, to hear those ambitious words! Since that day, Matteo had written three secret notes to her about the wonders of Ancient Greece. She had read and re-read each of those notes many times, always feeling a lurch inside. On the day that he had sent her a poem filled with mythic metaphors that confused as much as they enthralled, Annalisa's heart had leapt and sang.

Was it possible? she wondered. *Matteo and I, betrothed?* He was near-enough a man and she was only a few months off entering her fifteenth year. As far as she knew or could guess, she would soon be deemed available. But would her father be ready—and willing—to agree to such a union? Or were there other plans not yet revealed?

'Wake up! Anna, wake up!'

Her mother, shouting across the fetid carriage. Reluctantly, Annalisa opened her eyes.

'We're here,' said Carlotta de Torriano.

The villa had been built close to the crest of one of the smaller hills. Annalisa's father had previously announced that the view from the *loggia*, across a succession of shallow hills and valleys that sat below a dark forest, was magnificent and, for once, it was difficult to disagree. Even the most reluctant visitor could appreciate the rolls of verdant countryside and the prettiness of the distant orchards that lay beneath a sky which was—she had to admit—delightfully blue.

Near the *loggia* there was a stone well, reachable by wide steps, then a semi-circle of lawn, and a garden made for herbs—Annalisa spotted basil, fennel, coriander and sage—and ornamental flowers. She was further forced to admit to herself that the fountain in the middle of the lawn was impressive—a strong flow of crystal water gushing from the mouths of contorting beasts and impassive angels—and that her bedroom was spacious and full of light. Even the *lunette* over the doorway was pretty.

Despite such positives, however, this was not a time for blank acceptance. Her family needed to understand that her misgivings about coming to the *contado* were important, that *she* was important! She supervised Martina's unpacking—*Why was the girl so slow?*—then returned to the *loggia*, where her mother was checking a list of fruits bound for the preserving jars.

Annalisa sighed.

No response. She took an extra couple of steps and sighed again.

'Anna,' said her mother in a recognisably dangerous voice, 'understand this. We are here and we are not leaving.'

'But, Mother—'

'Did you not hear me? Should I repeat myself?'

'I did hear you, but—'

'Impossible child!' Carlotta's eyes drilled into her. 'Why must you greet every turnaround in your life, no matter how minor, with such drama? Look about you—'

'I have looked.'

'Look *properly* and see how fortunate we are, how fortunate *you* are to have a father who has worked hard and courted success!'

'I miss Florence!'

'You'd miss Rome, too, if we lived there. Or France, or the moon, or the bottom of the ocean. The place is irrelevant.'

'Mother, no!'

'Daughter, yes. You are determined to be miserable, because in your mind what you had before will always be better than what you have now. If you were a poor serving-girl, with a single set of clothes and nothing but black bread to eat, and we took you in and gave you the best dresses and the most delicious food, you'd still complain about having to change your ways. It is the height of selfishness and I won't have it!'

Annalisa knew that her mother was rarely angered, but when it happened, those on the receiving end were like soldiers scaling the battlements, either shot down or roasted in oil. Very few made the parapet.

Experience suggested that it was better for her to gracefully withdraw—for now. She shifted the set of her face and said, more civilly, 'Mother, I am sorry. I will amend my behaviour.'

'Do so.' Carlotta opened her arms. 'Anna,' she said more warmly, 'let us enjoy our time here. Already I have heard of pleasantries. A well-known local family is hosting a performance tomorrow evening in the village and, happily, we are invited. So, please, do not dwell on Florence. I, for one, am relieved to be away from all of that posturing for a while.'

CHAPTER 2

Falling and Climbing

Thirteen-year-old Dante Bellomo gazed at the top of the oak tree, looked into the future, and said to his beloved friend, 'I can't do it.'

'Yes, you can!'

Dante bit his lip. 'Up there?' he said. 'Leo, I'm sorry. I really can't.'

They were standing in the garden that adjoined Leo's uncle's villa, away from the pond, overlooking the hills and olive orchards. Leo had chosen this as the site for his performance because of the formation of the trees. Apparently, the old oak sitting amid a line of cypresses had made him think of the Almighty watching kindly over players—'Like us, Dante!' More tellingly, the area on the opposite side sloped upwards into grassy tiers, like broad steps, which Leo saw as perfect for the large, enthusiastic audience that would doubtless attend.

Now he touched Dante lightly on the arm.

'You *can* do it,' he said.

'No, I can't.'

'I think differently, and so should you.'

'Leo, please. I can't do it!'

'You can, Dante, of course you can! Here, let me show you how.'

'No—'

'When you're ready, follow me, okay?'

As usual, he did not wait for an answer. Dante watched as his friend swung his athletic body onto the lowest branch, then scrambled up, his hands and feet as strong and assured as those of a lizard or a bear. Once at the midpoint, Leo straddled a thin-looking branch that quivered nervously, cupped his hands around his mouth and called out, 'You see? And you don't even have to go the whole way! Here is perfect!'

Dante lowered his head and bit his lip. The conflict in his heart was familiar, but no less painful for that. Leo could make him feel happy to the point of exhilaration, but also, without intending to do so, dismayed by what Dante saw as his own plentiful inadequacies.

A confident friend, he thought, *is a blessing, but also a reminder of your own meekness.*

He considered what they were going to do. Leo's performance was typically grand in its conception, and therefore typically difficult to execute. Dante recalled their conversation, only two days before.

'I have permission! Uncle Francesco said yes!'

'Permission for what, Leo?'

'Did I not tell you? We are staging a performance!'

'We are? *We*?'

'Yes, on Friday night, in the garden. I have already written invitations to every house in the village and beyond. Giacomo will ride them out this afternoon. Are you certain that I did not tell you?'

You rarely tell me, Dante thought, but he did not want to undermine his friend's enthusiasm. Besides, what harm could it do? Leo would organise everything and be everything, while he, Dante, stayed at the back, in the shadows, watching and supporting. *That is the way*, he thought. *The good way . . . not all of us can be* that *person. And none of us can be Leonardo.*

He knew that his friend was waiting for him to ask, so he did.

'What's it about?'

An apocalypse, Leo had told him. Dante was not surprised. Leo was fond of large-scale, cataclysmic events: storms and fires, earthquakes, huge stones falling mercilessly from the sky.

'A great flood!'

'I see. Then you will be Noah, building an ark?'

'No.' Suddenly, Leo was coy. 'Not him. Not that.'

'But what else—'

'We will begin with a procession of masks,' Leo said, making shapes in the air with his hands. 'Each mask will represent a cardinal sin.'

'That means there will be seven! Do you even have time—'

'Do not fret, Dante. I will ensure that the masks are prepared and they will be both functional and marvellous. Now, you will parade the masks—'

'Me?'

'Yes, my dear friend, you! I will be singing an original composition and playing on my lyre. Even I cannot simultaneously sing, play and walk around with seven masks in my hands. Dante, it must be you.'

That familiar queasiness crept like a rat towards his throat. Dante gulped.

'And then?' he asked.

'I deliver the script.'

'About?'

'The flood, of course, skilfully described as punishment for those sins. I will stand amid a ring of flaming torches and relate what happens in great detail.' He smiled engagingly and said, 'The audience will be afraid.'

I am already afraid, thought Dante. Standing within a ring of fire and proclaiming punishment sounded decidedly pagan. Some of those watching would surely be disturbed by such a sight.

'Are you listening?' Leo asked. Dante could see that he was becoming impatient, another regular trait.

'Yes. Sorry.'

'You realise what must happen next?'

'Yes. That is—no.'

'The world shall be saved!'

Good, thought Dante. He was relieved. God would appear in some appropriate form and the audience would realise—

'By a giant!'

Ah. Suddenly, Leo's earlier words made sense.

Not him. Not that.

'I will be wearing the giant's mask,' Leo told him, 'and I will light more torches, making a total of seven. You see the connection? Meanwhile, having dispensed with the masks, you will have climbed the oak tree.'

'But I told you—'

'When the seventh torch is lit and the fire is roaring into the night sky, I will bellow the giant's creed: *Le persone devono rispettare la natura*!'

People must respect nature. It was a familiar Leo sentiment, thought Dante.

'And from up in the trees, you will release the coloured leaves!'

'What coloured leaves?'

'The ones that I have already prepared and placed in a bag. Since the day before yesterday, in anticipation of my uncle's goodwill, I have been collecting dead leaves and painting them every colour of the rainbow and with the tints of every metal. They are spectacular!'

'I'm sure.'

'You will throw them out as if you were sprinkling

rose petals over the bodies of the departed. They will fall gently into the firelight, twinkling and reflecting as they turn, and our audience will know that the flood has been vanquished—'

Your audience, thought Dante, though not unkindly.

'—and the world is once again in a state of balance, as it should be.'

Nearby, a wood pigeon clucked and fussed. Leo winked at the bird.

'Naturally,' he said, 'there will be significant applause.'

Now Leo was insisting that Dante practise climbing the oak tree. Feeling that he could not disappoint his friend, Dante did his best, clambering awkwardly up and over the first branch, before he couldn't help himself and looked down.

And froze.

It wasn't the distance, which he knew to be relatively small. What frightened him was the idea of falling. Throughout his short life, he had endured nightmares in which he had seen himself plummeting from a white light to the most complete darkness. This fall was headlong and irreversible, with nothing to delay or distract him, no bumps or obstructions, no colours or lights and no sounds, not even his own screams of terror. He would hurtle down, down—until, inexplicably, he would awaken, bedclothes awry, body slicked with sweat, mind still reeling from the agony of what had just happened as he tried to settle the thump of his heart. But as he slowly recovered, Dante would be left with the thought that while falling was bad enough, the greater horror lay in wondering if this lonely fate was only ever dreamed by those who were unloved and unlikely to be missed, those whose fate was eternal irrelevance.

He'd been too scared to tell anyone about these visitations: not his father, who only cared for the money that he craved each morning and the drink that he craved each evening; nor his mother, who was tired all the time; and certainly not his grandmother, Ludovica. He knew exactly what she would say, not just to him but to everyone.

'It's a sign! He's cursed! That boy is cursed!'

His peace-keeping mother would pretend to agree with Ludovica, as she always did. His father, openly indifferent to matters of faith or the spirit, would be more pragmatic.

'Dreams are nothing!' Stefano Bellomo would scoff. 'You hear me? Nothing!' Then he would limp to the table, take another cup of wine and stare at them all with his piercing eyes before uttering the familiar refrain, 'Tell me, anyone, tell me—'

Tell you?

'What am I going to do with this son of mine?'

CHAPTER 3

Revelation

Quickly, despite her misgivings, Annalisa became accustomed to life in the countryside.

The smell was different to that of Florence. The city's main odours came from people and their activities, the sweat and grime raised by the dawn-to-dusk striving of masons, builders, lawyers and traders, and from money being made, exchanged, lost, remade and ultimately invested, as her father had done, in the Monte de Pieta, the state bank. But here, on the outskirts of Vinci, all of that was gone. Instead, Annalisa found herself able to smell the rich offerings of the soil and also the energy beneath that soil, as if the mysterious fires that burned in the middle of the earth were sending their smoke through unseeable cracks to remind humanity: *down here, we continue. Build your cities, play your money games, send out your ships, fight your wars, but we will continue, always.*

There were other smells, too. The wind carried the

scents of the cherries, mulberries, peaches and plums that appeared as clusters of colour in the orchards that sprawled generously over the lower valleys. Taking its own turn, the sunlight extracted perfumes from the many patches of wild oregano and thyme, and from the armies of flowers that marched in the fields: the poppies, cyclamen, anemones and, Annalisa's favourite, the lilac crocuses.

The smell of animals was ever present; the horses, goats and sheep, of course, but also those beasts that lived secretly and, she hoped, sedately in the forests. Vanni had mentioned foxes and deer, but it was Luca who, having seen Anna walk onto the lawn below the *loggia*, had raced down and insisted that boars roamed the nearby forest, as well as other wild animals, even the lynx.

'Do you know what such an animal eats, Anna?'

'No,' she'd said, deliberately feigning indifference because Luca's eyes were already gleaming with mischievous intent. Annalisa's second brother was not especially Florentine in style, but his devilish nature did appeal to many people, her included.

'Squirrels,' he'd told her. He'd used his fingers to mimic a squirrel scuttling along before it was whooshed into eternity. 'Rabbits. A marmot or two.'

'That is the way of the world.'

'Indeed. But listen, sweet sister, and listen well, because you need to hear this. It is a well-known fact that, if the opportunity presents, the lynx prefers the taste of *human* flesh.'

Annalisa had felt a tiny jolt of fear, but shaken her head. 'That cannot be. Our father would not allow us to come to a place where such a danger exists.'

'Oh, it's true alright. This is a predator that's as cunning and treacherous as a Sienese spy. I have it on good authority that our lynx is especially fond of consuming young ladies.'

'You're lying!'

'Go for a walk. See if I am.'

'Perhaps I will,' she'd told him. 'I'm not scared.'

'Good luck.' Her brother had grinned. 'You won't hear a thing, until suddenly—'

He'd flopped down and pretended to die horribly, making Annalisa laugh. With Luca, it had always been difficult to remain serious.

That evening, Carlotta and her children travelled to the village, where they were ushered into the gardens of a villa owned by a man named Francesco da Vinci. He was dark-haired, with a hooked nose and a slight stoop. He greeted the Torrianos warmly and directed them towards chairs and benches placed on grassy tiers that were illuminated by several torches. Further down, more torches created a brighter patch of light between the grass and some trees.

As servants handed out cups of wine, Carlotta, Vanni, Luca and Annalisa were politely acknowledged by other holidaying Florentines, mostly the families of well-known merchants such as Signors Moretti, Bonocchi and Volpe, and they were introduced to dignitaries from the village, including the mayor, a black-toothed individual by the name of Aiello. People were jovial and talkative. Annalisa saw a stout man stumble into the light and heard him shout across the lawn.

'Francesco, greetings! What's this about, anyway?'

'Signor Fallaci, you pest of pests, who allowed you in?'

'Your cook, of course. She wants to test her wares on someone with a proper appetite.'

'Do you mean her *kitchen* wares, old rascal?'

'Francesco, of course! What decent man would speak of wares other than those offered from the kitchen?' There was a flurry of laughter, then the stout man said, as much to the audience as to his host, 'Tell us, good sir, are we to be held captive by yet another of Leonardo's dire fictions?'

'My nephew is a boy of great creativity and intellect,' Francesco told him. 'I am sure we will all be hugely entertained.'

The stout man laughed and danced a ridiculous jig that made others laugh with him. At that point, platters of *formaggio* were served, the pungent cheese ringed by figs, cherries and sweet almonds. The audience continued their conversations as they ate and drank, and Annalisa could hear phrases popping like bubbles off water.

'Two *florins*, two!'

'Promised me the finest cotton and failed to deliver . . .'

‘Signor Conti, of course, the old charlatan . . .’

‘I hear that the boy insists on visiting his mother, despite her being a mere peasant *and* married to someone else . . .’

‘Should be a straightforward commission, however . . .’

‘I fear the poor beast’s lameness which, as we know, means . . .’

‘A brace of pigeons, several hares . . .’

In the shadows at the bottom of the hill, a small girl with a pale face was patiently lacing daisies. Annalisa wondered if the girl was lost.

She looked around. Vanni and Luca were immersed in the crowd, no doubt organising their own amusements. Carlotta, included briefly in an animated discussion with three other women, turned to her daughter and said, ‘You see how wonderful life in the country can be?’

But Annalisa saw the hard glitter in her mother’s eyes, saw how her lips had already settled into the unreadable expression of a major guildsman’s wife.

Suddenly, a drumbeat and a flourish. She looked to the circle of light. The performance was about to begin.

She was late to bed that night. She lay beneath her coverlet, listening as the last traces of wind eased the land towards sleep, and thought about what she had just seen. Such a strange event! It had begun with masks, all wondrous creations but unsettling with their exaggerated features and bold colours. As the masks were paraded, a golden-haired boy had emerged from the darkness. The boy had played a lyre and sung, and it had been enchanting, each note from his pure voice soaring as if he alone were a choir and the stellar sky his cathedral. She'd been rapt in the boy's singing, but utterly transfixed when he had stepped further into the light to deliver a speech, and she'd seen how handsome he was. No, *handsome* was the wrong word; his features had been woven by an artisan with the deftest touch and could not be described in such a masculine manner. Now, she settled the matter in her mind. *That boy is beautiful*, she thought, *as a dove is beautiful, and so too the curling head of a rose.*

There had been unease among the audience when the final mask had been revealed. Was this ugly and ridiculous figure supposed to be an ogre? A god from one of the ancient civilisations? Annalisa had been uncertain. She'd overheard Vanni saying to Luca, 'Bold or stupid, do you think?' Her brother's reply, if uttered, had been swallowed by the murmuring.

More torches, a proclamation about nature, then came a lighter moment, enjoyed—and probably needed, she'd thought—by the audience. A smaller boy, pretty in his own way, but pallid and scared looking, had been jammed into a fork on the main tree. While the audience had tittered, the boy had cried out, 'Leo, I can't go any higher!' There'd been some sort of exchange before the boy in the tree had thrown a bag onto the grass below. Unperturbed, the main boy had emerged from his hiding place, picked up the bag, opened it, dipped in his hands and tossed the contents of the bag into the air. Suddenly, he and his golden locks were standing amid a rain-shower of sparkle and colour. Annalisa had been unable to stop herself from thinking that this beautiful human had looked as divine and serene as those figures from the frescoes within the Church of Santa Maria: Orcagna's saints, kneeling before Christ.

Now, she rolled over, faced the slanting moonlight, and put her hand beneath her cheek. *Yes*, she thought sleepily. *That was it—that was her revelation.* This boy, this brilliant, shining-lantern of a boy, had stepped out of a painting. But not one created by Orcagna. Not one created by Masaccio either, or Giotto or Verrocchio. She knew it as clearly as she had known anything during her time on Earth: this young man, this Leonardo, had stemmed directly from the brushwork of God.

CHAPTER 4

Heart and Soul

Dante considered the events of the evening.

As tended to happen, Leo had been widely praised after the performance—although not, sadly, by his father, who, since the untimely death of his wife Albiera, rarely left Florence. But Uncle Francesco, always a strong supporter, had marched down the slope, held Leo's arms high, and encouraged the audience's applause. Dante had been embarrassed but pleased to see Francesco acknowledge his own contribution by gesturing in his direction, but less impressed when many of the audience had laughed. Someone had even called out rudely, '*Complimenti, scimmia!*' *Congratulations, monkey.*

After which others had crowded around: friends, acquaintances and family such as Leo's Aunt Violante, who insisted on pinching Dante's cheeks and calling him *piccolo*—little one—and Accattabriga, the husband of Leo's mother, who'd been unable to attend.

‘Caterina is ill,’ Leo had explained earlier. ‘We will visit her when she is recovered.’

We will visit her. Dante knew that he was expected to tag along. That was his role, not that he minded. The alternative of staying at home was far less desirable. And Leo, who always treated him with kindness, had the ability to make Dante feel better by pushing aside his fears and laying out a more pleasant version of the world like a lavish picnic.

Last summer, Dante had dared to ask, ‘Leo, are we—’

That cherished word, so difficult to say.

‘Dear friend, are we what? Are we supreme? Are we fish?’

He’d grinned before swallowing hard and saying, ‘Are we . . . like brothers?’

Leo had mused for a moment.

‘No,’ he’d said.

Disappointment had settled like clay in Dante’s chest.

‘I’m sorry,’ he’d mumbled. ‘I didn’t—’

‘Brothers fight,’ Leo had told him, with an encouraging smile. ‘They compete to win affection from their parents. They scheme and they wrangle. Dante, brothers are, for the most part, terrible beasts filled with rage and envy. Who would want such a curse? No, we are better than mere brothers!’

‘Then we are friends?’

‘Better again. Dante, think of the human form. We each own a heart, agreed?’

'Of course.'

'And a soul?'

'Yes. Although—'

'You are thinking about evil. Dante, even the most terrible, afflicted beings have souls. However much life and circumstances might have damaged those poor instruments, they continue to exist.'

'If you say so.'

'I do say so, and you know that I am invariably correct. So, a heart and a soul. A Leo and a Dante, and a Dante and a Leo. Independent but connected, each unable to properly exist without the other.'

Dante recalled the pleasure of that moment, knowing that he was as significant and vital as anything or anyone else in the world. But that was Leo's gift: to give him worthwhileness by finding him a comfortable, and comforting, place within the grandeur.

While Leo had celebrated the performance with whoever would join him, Dante had wandered through the crowd and been surprised to hear some negative comments. One man had said loudly, 'Piero's boy is vain enough to fire his arrows at sacred targets,' and Dante had heard another man suggest to his friends that Leo's work was disjointed.

'These tricks and lyrics are pleasing to the eye and to the ear,' said the man, 'but what is the point of it all?'

'No point,' replied one of his companions gruffly, 'beyond the stoking of the young master's reputation.'

'Ah, yes,' agreed another. 'If self-promotion is a talent, then Leonardo is more talented than most.'

After people had dispersed, some going home, others floating like fireflies into the villa, the boys had begun to pack up with the assistance of Giacomo and another servant. Leo had been chattering excitedly about the audience's appreciation of his performance when Dante, remembering, said to him, 'There was a girl.'

'Dante, there were many girls. And boys, and ladies and men, and moths and butterflies, and ants, beetles, worms, skinks, salamanders and probably wolves, as well as ghosts, goblins, ogres, unicorns, perhaps even a centaur and its good friend, the dromedary, and so on. We had an audience of thousands.'

They were picking up the coloured leaves and putting them back in the bag.

Dante said, 'I meant, a new girl.'

'A new girl? Are you certain?'

'I know what a girl looks like.'

'Do you? Could she perhaps have been a new cat—'

'Leo—'

'Or a new angel, descended from the heavens so as to satisfy her earthly curiosity?'

Dante shook his head and said, 'Be serious. I only noticed her because she was staring.'

'They were all staring,' Leo told him. 'Brilliance draws the eye.'

Dante could not help but smile. 'Is there no end to

your ego?' he asked.

'None whatsoever. My ego travels across all lands. It is as dogged and expansive as the great Marco Polo. Now, describe this new girl-cat-angel to me. Was she good-looking? Did you fall in love like a hapless prince?'

Dante had laughed that away. The girl had been very still, he knew that much. A statue whose gaze had not varied, Leo being its sole focus.

The next morning, having completed his chores and gulped down a quick breakfast, Dante returned to the villa. Francesco had offered to take the boys riding. Dante was not confident with horses, but Leo had insisted that a skilled teacher like his uncle could make anyone a better rider.

'Come on! What's the worst thing that could happen?'

'I fall off and die.'

'Is that so bad? If you die, you will go to Heaven because there is no-one more virtuous than you, Dante Bellomo. God will see you coming and say to the Angel Gabriel, "Prepare the choir, here comes one of the best!" He will look after you and make you a special envoy with immense powers. Dante, your prospects are amazing!'

While Leo rode Francesco's preferred horse, a spirited bay, Dante sat on the oldest mare, with Leo's uncle seated behind him for support and encouragement.

They left the village and clopped steadily over the meadows, towards the forest. It was a glorious day, clear-skied and already warm. People in the orchards and fields waved as they passed and Dante's fears of falling and dying were quelled, if only temporarily.

On reaching the forest, they drifted into a lightly wooded hollow before finding a stream, dismounting and watering the horses. Leo, always thrilled by natural springs, asked his uncle if he and Dante might leave the horses and follow the stream on foot.

Francesco's gaze flickered back and forth. 'Follow it to where?' he asked.

'To the other side of the world, of course. Uncle, perhaps we will meet you there.'

'Why would I go to the other side of the world?'

'Because it exists. Why else?'

'Why else, indeed? Very well. If I am not at the other side of the world when you arrive, find your own way home, where I will be enjoying your dinners.'

Francesco linked the horses and led them away. Ever obedient, Dante followed Leo into the forest. The stream ran playfully, before a deepening bed made the flow more insistent and darkened the emerald water. The boys walked along the mossy bank, reaching a bend where Leo was entranced by a small inlet. He bent down, examined the water and said, 'See how the current curves?'

Knowing that it was his duty, Dante also bent down.

Leo said, 'There is a moment when all parts of the water unite and become like a curling hair. It is the exact same shape.' He pulled out the notebook and stub of red chalk that he always carried and began to draw the movement of the water, over and over, as if that shape needed perfecting.

'Dante!'

'Mm?'

'Watch as the light strikes the top of the water—see how it dances!'

Dante could not spot any dancing light, but he knew from experience that it was best to agree. Leo continued to draw frantically. When the sketches were done to his satisfaction, he tucked the notebook and chalk into his belt and the boys trudged further upstream, towards a distant humming sound. As they progressed, the track became more difficult because of the density of the vegetation and the slipperiness of the rocks that lined the banks.

Dante, struggling for breath, gasped, 'How much further?'

Leo raised his hand. 'Listen!'

Dante realised that the humming had become a deep-chested roar. Was the world moving? Expanding and compressing like an enormous set of bellows? He looked around nervously and saw that Leo, who'd moved ahead, was pointing through the trees.

'A cataract!'

They came out of the green into a flute of gold-grey light and the blessing of the sky. Water cascaded from a small cliff, forming a natural swimming hole amid a church of rocks. Already, Leo was ripping off his clothes.

'Come on!' he cried.

He was brightly naked when he tumbled into the dark water, his slicked head emerging quickly and bobbing across the froth like an elegant bird. Dante, more tentative, squatted on a rock and sifted the water through his fingers.

The stream ran fast as the forest hummed with life's most thrilling energies. Dante dipped both hands into the coolness. Leo's shouts of joy echoed and rose. Neither boy saw the figure in the trees beyond, watching them.

CHAPTER 5

Exploration

Annalisa awoke late and completed her prayers with more haste and less attention than her parents would have considered appropriate. The villa was silent, the mid-morning air already laden with heat. Walking from room to room felt like pushing through a maze.

She ate some cherries from a bowl and went outside to the shimmering flagstones. Her mother was resting in her favourite *curule* chair, placed carefully in an area where the shade would be day long. Vanni and Luca had instructed the servants, before riding into the village to purchase provisions and meet with new friends, while Alessandro, Annalisa's father, was still in the city, fostering partnerships and making deals, making money.

Always money.

She stood near a statue of Bacchus and a faun and said, 'What will I do now?'

When Carlotta did not answer, Annalisa asked

petulantly, 'Mother? Did you hear my question?'

'I heard.'

'Then tell me please, what will I—'

'Try staying quiet,' her mother told her.

'I am quiet.'

'Are you? Then that shrill and persistent sound that I hear must be an insect, not your voice.'

A brief silence until Carlotta said, 'Anna, why not practise your embroidery?'

'I hate embroidery.'

'Do you? That is new.'

'No—'

'Last week you told me how much you loved the art.'

'I did not say *loved*.'

'Words to that effect. Are you now reconsidering your whims on a week-to-week basis? As your parent, it would be useful to know this, Anna.'

'No, Mother.'

'Then—'

'I have always hated embroidery! It is time-wasting for dullards.'

'Really? I must remember that, next time I have a needle between my fingers. Very well, if embroidery is beneath you, read your Latin and improve your wit.'

Annalisa rubbed her fingers over Bacchus's elegant calf muscle.

She murmured, 'I am witty enough and I hate Latin only slightly less than I hate embroidery.'

Her mother's gaze suddenly became very direct.

'Daughter,' she said, 'boldness should never be mistaken for intelligence. It is a poor relation that all too frequently outstays its welcome.'

'But—'

'Need I also remind you of the importance of developing a learned mind? Your father has been very clear about that.'

Annalisa was well aware of the implication that lay behind her mother's words. The Florentine mantra was precise: well-read young ladies were more likely to attract well-bred—and potentially wealthy—young men.

Matteo?

She sighed loudly, to no effect. The conversation with her mother was obviously over and, frustratingly, she had made little headway. Irritated, she picked up a book—Alighieri's *Purgatorio*—and pretended to read.

Time dragged. The manuscript blurred. Annalisa heard a bee hovering, swatted the insect away and glanced towards her mother's chair.

Carlotta de Torriano had closed her eyes. She was breathing deeply . . . snoring gently.

When she was satisfied that her mother was asleep, Annalisa slid the book beneath a cushion and quietly ventured away from the *loggia*. Earlier that morning, on the outer cusp of dawn, she'd awoken briefly to whispers of light rain floating across the countryside. The calming effect of that rain had been very different from what she was used to. City rain was filthy, like a street puddle tipped upside-down. It extracted the stench of history from the city's stones. She'd never told anyone in her family—undoubtedly, they would have scoffed—but for Annalisa the rain in Florence smelled like blood-spill.

At least Matteo had taken her seriously. They'd been sneaking away from the Medici's extravaganza when a storm had unexpectedly broken. The nearest shelter had been the chapels on the Ponte di Rubaconte. Matteo had rushed her into the shadows and from there they'd watched huge squalls ripping holes in the Arno. Feeling daring, Annalisa had shared her theory and been thrilled when Matteo had nodded as if in confirmation of her wisdom.

'Florence has a skin,' he'd shouted, 'and it is a pretty skin that everyone wants to gaze upon and caress. But beneath any skin—'

'Lies blood.' She'd smiled demurely, the sharing of an idea more pleasing than she could have imagined. Matteo had touched her fingertips for the second time, leaned close to her ear and repeated in a low, intense voice, 'It is a pretty skin . . . a pretty skin indeed.'

At which point the deluge had eased and they'd been able to leave the bridge and scamper unseen back to the festival. Now Annalisa was in the *contado*, thinking about the gentle coaxing of the early rain and finding an unexpected joy in the awakening of the grass and recolouring of the flowers, their hues already potent enough to sting her eyes. She blinked as she scanned the hills and saw workers moving towards their crops, goats and sheep quietly grazing, and, in the distance, a pair of horses and their riders trotting along the perimeter of the mysterious forest.

Oh yes, she thought defiantly. *Yes!* This was not a day for embroidery or the grim tales of Signor Alighieri: this was a day for exploration! She was new in this place. Should she not discover how life unfolded beyond the entrapment of the villa's hedges and walls?

Would her mother mind?

The answer was obvious: only if she knew.

Annalisa passed through a side gate, crossed the grassy contours and followed a path along the upper brow of the land. Her progress was slowed marginally by the need to keep her *cioppa* free of nettles and weeds. When she reached the nape of the next hill, she paused to look west towards the unseen ocean that Luca insisted he would one day conquer and was rewarded with a rush of blue light skimming across the deeply tinted landscape.

A swallow landed nearby, glanced over and wobbled its head inquisitively. Annalisa said hello, pulled out a grass stalk and gently reached over, as if to tickle the bird's wings. The swallow's eyes gleamed with what she hoped was appreciation for her kindness before it unlatched its wings and returned to the sky. Annalisa watched the swallow's progress until it vanished in the glare. The bird had made her feel unusually happy, almost to the point of tears.

She continued to push through the fierce heat towards the forest. *It would be cooler there*, she thought, *and exciting*, for she had never set foot inside such a heavily treed area. Her standard explorations were of streets and marketplaces, or inside the magnificent, glittering rooms of the *palazzi*, to which her parents were occasionally invited.

Picking her way through longer grass and clusters of wild daffodils, she reached the twisting oaks and maples. There was no obvious path, but here, on the rim of the forest, the trees were far enough apart to allow her entrance. Suppressing her fear of the unknown, Annalisa trod into the half-light. The sponginess of the leaf-litter and the pretty patches of orange and yellow lichen on the tree bark relaxed her, and the milder, sweeter air made her think that she was sniffing the remnants of ancient breezes, trapped for all time beneath those giant canopies of leaves.

Deep within the forest, she found a stream and walked alongside it until she reached a glade where the trees had parted enough to allow in sunshine. The light touching the water sent mirages into the forest's most secret pockets, and the stream wound on, eventually bisecting a stone plateau and turning into an inky torrent that plunged over the edge of a precipice.

Annalisa wondered about the water's final destination. Did it continue its journey through the forest or disappear into the undercarriage of the Earth? Did it head towards the sea? She looked around and saw that there was a track snaking down one side of the precipice. Following such a path would surely help her to find an answer to her question, but she guessed that the track would be slippery and there might be beasts hidden in the thickets, even the lynx that Luca had spoken of.

Embroidery? Books? An improved wit? Much better to learn of the world through experience!

No longer caring about her dress—the hem was filthy but Martina could fix that—she took to the track and scrambled down, pausing to watch the water tumble onto a rocky base then regather itself in a pearly haze and flow into a pool.

A pool where—

Voices? Yes, and they were familiar. Annalisa looked across and saw two boys, a small one sitting by the side of the pool with his back to her, the other, larger boy splashing about in the water.

'Dante,' yelled the latter, 'come in!'

'I can't swim!'

'I'll teach you!'

'Leo, no. I can't—'

'Dante, you can! I will teach you and you will become a mighty fish, a Leviathan to challenge Neptune himself!'

When the larger boy paddled towards the edge of the pool, Annalisa realised why she had known the voice: the owner had orchestrated last night's performance.

As he arose from the water, she spied his golden locks and impudent smile, then she realised that he was not wearing a shirt—not wearing anything! Flushing at the prospect of what she might see, she turned away, but not before a gust of laughter had escaped her mouth and taken flight.

CHAPTER 6

Rocks and Water

'Leo, did you hear that?'

'I can hear you.'

'Not me, that sound!'

'There are many sounds, Dante. I open my ears in this majestic palace and hear the insects babbling, the water frolicking, the clouds moving—'

'Not even *you* can hear the clouds!'

'Oh, but I can. They whisper their secrets to me. Clouds are fine communicators and useful observers, given that they may scan the world in its entirety. Dante, if you want to know more about different countries and the strange habits of humans, just ask a cloud.' He was pulling on his chemise without hurry or concern.

Dante said, with greater insistence, 'Leo, I heard someone laugh!'

'A good thing, surely,' Leo told him. 'In today's world, the few who laugh provide a welcome balance to the many who are devoted to being endlessly serious.' He buttoned his tunic, slicked back his hair, sat next to the worried-looking Dante and said, 'Dear friend, look around us. These rocks are serious, are they not? I doubt that any rock would ever laugh! By contrast, this water is light-hearted. It froths and bubbles. Now, imagine what would happen if there were no rocks. The water would soak, unseen and unheard, into the earth. Equally, imagine if there was no water. The rocks would sit for centuries, while all around them nothing would grow. You see how it works? Each needs the other. The light-hearted water runs across the serious rocks, plants and animals benefit, balance is maintained, life continues.'

'Yes, but—'

Leo grinned, clasped Dante's shoulder and said in a low voice, 'Don't worry. You're not going mad. I too heard someone laugh.' He stood, took a few steps away from the pool and called out, 'I am Leonardo, King of the Forest, and this fearsome *guerriero* is my military adviser and protector, the Great Bellomo. We demand that you show yourself!'

There was no reply. Dante stared into the deep, undulating greenness.

He said, 'Perhaps we imagined, a bird or a rat—'

But Leo ignored him and called again in the resounding voice of the crier, 'Show yourself to the King of the Forest, you ghastly apparition, or be warned, the Great Bellomo will seek you out. He may look like the gentlest creature alive, but do not be fooled! His vengeance is terrifying!'

'Leo, please!'

'Once provoked, he will rip the legs off running tigers! His stare can turn the dragon's fire to ice and his fingers have been known to pluck the eyes from an eagle as it dives for its prey! So, do not cross the Great Bellomo for he is mightier than Jupiter, and meaner and smarter than Hercules was when he crushed Antaeus!'

Still no reply. Leo continued to scan the trees. Neither boy moved for what seemed like an age—the water stilled, the world gone silent—until both heard the rustling of leaves coming from the higher ground to the side of the cataract.

A hand, a shoe, a hem, a glimpse of thickly corded hair. Finally, a girl emerged from the green.

'O Great Bellomo,' said Leo quietly, 'this is neither a bird nor a rat.'

But Dante had already recognised the watcher from last night's performance. As she eased down the slope, he guessed that the girl was of a similar age to them. Her skin was darker than was usual for people of the area, and the guarded look on her face spoke of both guile and defiance. Her black hair was tightly bound except for some stray ringlets that bobbed around her face, and she was wearing a magenta overdress, torn at the base. As she came into the light, Dante saw that she moved carefully, but with significant resolve. He sensed that any person who dared to rise up against this girl would be swiftly and decisively vanquished.

Finally, she stood opposite: glowering, calculating.

'I offer my apologies,' she said. Her voice was low, but very clear. 'I did not intend to spy on you. I was—' She compressed her lips slightly and glanced at the pool. 'I was enchanted by the water.'

'Or were you enchanted by what was *in* the water?' Leo asked, bringing a furious colour to the girl's face.

Feeling sorry for her, Dante inched closer.

'My friend likes to tease,' he said. 'My name is Dante Bellomo and this newly crowned king is Leonardo da Vinci.' The girl acknowledged his manners before Dante added, 'I believe that I may have seen you at Leo's performance last night.'

'Aha!' said Leo. 'Behold: the girl-cat-angel!'

Her eyes flashed, but she nodded at Dante and said, 'I am Annalisa de Torriano and you are correct, my family was there. It was a kind invitation. My father has recently acquired a villa in this area so we . . . we . . .' She seemed to run out of words, before adding, 'Anyway, my mother insisted.'

'I have two mothers,' said Leo, 'neither of whom insists.'

Now Annalisa stared at him, openly curious.

'How can that be?'

'How can what be? Your question must be specific, Annalisa de Torriano, or I will tire myself out by thinking of a thousand possible answers.'

At last she smiled; the effect was illuminating.

'Forgive me, Leonardo—King. You said *two* mothers?'

'Correct. I am either greedy or needy; you may take your pick.'

'I will pick neither and simply say that having two mothers seems unusual.'

'Only to those who are unlucky enough to have but one.'

'That is a fair point—'

'Made by a fair man.'

'And fairly put. But I must ask, how is it that you can have double the usual quantity of mothers and yet remain free from insistence?'

'Free from *their* insistence, not *all* insistence. Despite my unusual parental situation, I must insist that I am well-insisted.'

Annalisa smiled again.

She said, 'And well-considered too—'

'Of course—'

'At least, in your own estimation.'

Leo's laughter crackled high into the leaves.

'And why not?' he crowed. 'My talents are considerable!'

'That is of little use,' said Annalisa, 'if you lack consideration.' The embarrassment in her face had abated and her eyes were sparkling.

Leo turned to Dante.

'Good friend,' he said, 'this Cataract Creature has wit and grit. I propose that she be admitted to our Royal Palace—'

'I have no desire to become a queen to your king, if that is your proposal—'

'In equal partnership.'

'Equal,' echoed Annalisa. 'In that case, I accept your offer with all the graciousness that it may or may not deserve, although on one proviso.'

'She has the mind of a lawyer! What is your proviso?'

'That the King of the Forest remembers to wear his clothes whenever he returns to his realm.'

Again, Leo laughed.

'I am happy to grant you that,' he said. 'Welcome to our *palazzo*, Annalisa de Torriano.'

'I have been to real *palazzi* in Florence,' she told him primly, 'and this place is—'

'Richer in spirit, with air that is actually breathable.' Leo performed an elaborate bow, before offering his hand in the manner of a man concluding a deal. Annalisa grasped his fingers and they shook, while Dante, still dazzled by their rapid-fire exchange, watched on.

'I should go,' said Annalisa. 'As well as insisting that we attend every available social occasion, my mother must also know where I am and who I am with at all times.'

'Then you may satisfy her curiosity,' said Leo, 'by telling her that you have been jousting with a king.'

This time, Annalisa's laughter seemed to catch in the

light like mysterious, heavenly bells.

She was readying herself to climb the side of the cataract when Leo said, 'A moment?'

She stopped.

'Yes?'

'I wanted to say: Annalisa de Torriano, you have a near perfect smile.'

Once again, that curious gaze.

'Good control of your lips,' he told her. 'Either you were born with remarkably strong mouth-muscles or you are a frequent and enthusiastic smiler.'

This time, Annalisa was taken aback.

'Why do you say such a thing?' she asked.

'Because I study smiles. Dante will tell you that I study many things, but I am especially interested in smiles. My goal is to one day paint the perfect smile.'

'Then you plan to be an artist?'

'I plan nothing. I become an artist when I draw, just as I become a player when I play and a designer when I design.' He was looking at her as openly and scientifically as if he were appraising the structure of a building or a bridge. 'Perhaps,' he said, 'when I choose to paint the perfect smile, I may use your lips as a model?'

'You said "near perfect",' Annalisa reminded him. 'Such a judgment means that my smile is not ready for modelling.'

'Not ready *yet*,' Leo told her mysteriously—and he smiled.

CHAPTER 7

Repentance

Energised by her meeting in the forest, Annalisa quickly reached the tiny chapel that marked the boundary of the estate—and was shocked to see the family's best stallion being led across the villa's forecourt by old Ferrando.

The stallion that only one person was permitted to ride.

Annalisa tightened her dress into folds so that the rips and stains would be less obvious and hurried to the side of the building, where, earlier, she had spied a back entrance. She squeezed open the door, willing it not to creak, and thought, *if I can slip through the kitchen and bypass the central courtyard that leads to the* loggia—

'Where have you been?'

Her father's bulk dominated the far end of the room. When he was in a good mood, Alessandro often patted his ample belly and referred jokingly to 'the weight of success'. One quick glance at his smouldering eyes confirmed that here, now, he was not in a good mood.

'Come with me,' he ordered.

He led Annalisa into the privacy of the parlour. The sun was filtered by wooden shutters, but the air in the room was no cooler than the air outside.

Alessandro turned. *Father was not an unreasonable man*, thought Annalisa, *more usually quite the opposite*. Giggly, flirtatious Cosetta called him *L'orso*, The Bear. However, like any Florentine father, he had firm expectations for his children.

She was not stupid. Rash, perhaps, but not stupid. She knew that by leaving the villa with no indication of her intentions or whereabouts, she would have worried her parents. Better, then, to be direct.

Hoping to head off the inevitable barrage of questions, she said, 'I was exploring. Father, I had an adventure! On such a warm and wonderful day, I was drawn to the outer world like . . . like iron to the lodestone.'

Silence.

So, she thought, *being direct is not enough. I must also be contrite.*

'However, I am sorry,' she told him. 'Terribly sorry.' She softened her features and her voice. 'I did not think and I did not check. My worst traits . . .'

Still nothing. She felt a trickle of perspiration run from the back of her neck. This unyielding heat—

'Exploring.' Alessandro's pronunciation made the word seem childish.

'Father, yes—'

'Yet I did not see you. I arrived here, happy to once again be reunited with my family, only to be told that you had disappeared. I rode over the hills and through the valleys, and you were nowhere. Vanni and Luca went into the village and they did not see you. You, a green girl, as vulnerable as she is naïve—vanished!'

He emphasised the word by slapping a wall with his open hand. Annalisa could barely breathe.

'So, tell me,' said her father, 'where or what were you *exploring*?'

'The forest,' she said.

Alessandro's dark eyes narrowed. He beckoned and she obeyed, coming close enough to smell the mustiness of his skin after a long day of toil and travel.

He said, 'You went to the forest?'

'Yes.'

'Alone?'

'I did not think that—'

'Answer my question, Anna.' He had not yet fully raised his voice, which she found disconcerting.

She bit her lip. Wandering alone in a forest, she would be justly punished for her foolish behaviour. But consorting in a forest with two unknown boys from the village . . .

She couldn't imagine.

'Yes,' she said. 'I was by myself.'

'And in making this decision, did you consider our

feelings?'

She shook her head and pretended to brush away a tear. Her father's nod was almost imperceptible.

'Did you consider your own safety?' He strode to the windows and pulled back the shutters, letting in the bright afternoon light. 'Look out there, Anna. Look where we are. This is no friendly *piazza*, no open street filled with familiar faces. We are in the *contado*. The tracks are lonely and often hidden from sight. There are bandits afoot, men who would cut a throat as easily as they cut a tomato for their supper. And what do you do? You go to the forest, alone and defenceless, a young girl with no experience of life's treacheries, no experience of wild animals—'

'I saw no animals,' said Annalisa, rising a little, 'unless you mean the pretty birds and kind spiders.'

'Do not interrupt me, child. Rather, think on this. As well as ignoring the wishes of your parents and jeopardising your own safety, you left the estate without a companion. What, then, of your honour? What of the Torriano honour and mine, as head of our family? Yes, we are here, but so are the eyes and ears of Florence. Do you wish for people to see you, see *us*, as dishonourable?'

Contrite, then, was not enough. Time for humility. She concentrated on further filling her eyes with tears.

'No,' she said. Her voice broke; her lips trembled.

Alessandro picked up a cup and drank deeply.

He said, 'Anna, I am a fair man, am I not?'

'Yes, Father.'

'Sufficiently fair to accept that, within reason, your time in the *contado* may be . . . less stringent than when we are in Florence. I would certainly like you to experience the delights of the orchards and fields, as well as the warm welcome offered by those families from the other villas and even, when appropriate, some of the more reputable people from the village. However, not—'

She waited.

'—*not* at the expense of your safety, nor your reputation for piety.' He took her by the chin, raised her face to his and offered her a glimmer of a smile, though it was more steel than silk. 'Anna,' he said, 'you are much loved, by many, and so it shall remain as long as you are thoughtful and obedient. Do you understand me?'

'Yes, Father.'

'You will not do this again? You will not bring shame upon our family?'

'No, Father.'

'Good. Then it is time for you to properly repent by making observances to our Lord. Come, the chapel awaits.'

Did he stay? Stand behind her to ensure her compliance? Head bowed, repeating the mantra from her *Book of Hours*, she could not tell

'"O Thou most sweet and loving Lord, Thou knowest mine infirmities and the necessities which I endure . . ."'

Later, she heard the chapel door open and close. Who was it? Were they arriving or departing? Or were they still there?

'"In great evils and sins, I am involved. I entreat of Thee consolation and support."'

'Anna,' said her mother's voice, 'you have been here long enough. God has surely listened.'

She raised her stricken face.

'Come.' Her mother's eyes were uncharacteristically tender.

Annalisa arose. Her knees were numb and there was pain in each elbow. They left the chapel and walked into the cooling air, the smell of cyclamen sawing across the breeze.

Inside the villa, Carlotta stopped Annalisa in the main hall.

'Your father has purchased a new painting,' she said proudly. 'It is small and a copy, however . . .' She paused before saying, 'Lovely, is it not?'

Annalisa recognised the red-cloaked figure. John the Baptist was alone in the wilderness with Brunelleschi's great dome painted behind him. The shaping of the saint's arms and the wind-bent trees formed a circle, with the distant city at its centre.

Carlotta indicated one of the trees in the painting. 'Look. There is an axe.'

'I see it.'

'Good. But, do you understand its significance?'

She hesitated.

'Mother, I am . . . uncertain.'

Carlotta said, 'Luke told us that every tree which does not bring good fruit will be cut down. Do you recall that passage?'

'No,' said Annalisa forlornly. 'I am lazy with Luke.'

Her mother's smile was restrained.

'Anna,' she said, 'do not punish yourself so. We are annoyed with you, but we are also realistic. We know that God did not create you to join the abbey. As your parents, we ask only that you behave more like a dutiful daughter than a wayward son. The Lord knows that Luca is trial enough. Give us some reprieve.'

Annalisa muttered her agreement.

Her mother ushered her closer to the painting.

'Now,' she said, 'the axe, the cutting down of those trees. Anna, you must understand; even here, in the *contado*, Florence intrudes. There are many who would love nothing more than to be critical of this family's fruit. Your brothers are older and they are men, meaning that they will be less affected. Whether this is fair or not is of no concern; it simply *is*. For you and me, however, the situation is different. On matters of reputation, we Torriano women cannot be too careful! As with anyone who ascends, your father has had to tread upon the egos of many who now crawl and carp beneath him. Some of these accept their fate, others are less forgiving. Do you understand what I am saying?'

She did. It was a form of condemnation, she thought bitterly. You are a girl, therefore your every word and action must be given in service to the reputation of your father and your brothers, then to your husband and your sons. Never disappoint. Never defy.

'Anna?'

'Mother,' she said, 'I understand. But I am very tired. May I go now?'

'Of course,' said Carlotta. 'Go, sleep.'

But as she went to her bed, Annalisa did not see the look that followed her, the soft-eyed sympathy of a fellow sufferer.

CHAPTER 8

Duty and Freedom

Ludovica relished the marketplace. She went every week, insisting that she needed to supervise Dante while he bought fresh fish for her faltering heart and a nice, plump partridge as a treat for what would no doubt be her final dinner on God's lamentable Earth. But Dante knew the real reason that his grandmother journeyed into Vinci. Ludovica wanted to gossip with her cronies, old Emilia and even older Dottorina.

For Dante, it was tiresome having to accompany her, however there was no escape. His father, who derived great pleasure from being rid of Ludovica's bellyaching for a few hours, had decided that one of Dante's household duties was to escort his tottering grandmother to the *piazza*, where she could sit with the other ladies, nibble on her favourite cheese tart and assess the passers-by.

'And that dolt is?'

'Muttiano, chief servant to Bordonaro, also a dolt.'

'Bordonaro, who wishes for his son to marry the daughter of the wool-merchant, D'Amato?'

'The same. Now, Bordonaro is Genoese—'

'Meaning that he is a fool?'

'Meaning that he has large debts.'

'Let me guess. The girl has a large dowry.'

'She does. Sadly, she is also as plain as a mule.'

'Dottorina, her unfortunate appearance is of little concern. It may, in fact, be of benefit.'

'How so?'

'The plain are rarely pursued. As a wife, she will have little choice but to be faithful.'

'Very true! And being a D'Amato means that she is likely to breed well.'

'The mule will become a rabbit, that's for certain. As such, I decree that theirs is a perfect match.'

'I agree. Now, Emilia, over there. Who is that, preening himself with the red feather?'

'That young bull? Zuccarelli, the currier's grandson.'

'Of course! What do we know of him?'

'A little, which is never enough. For example, you may not have heard that he was recently exiled from his father's home.'

'Really? Why was that?'

'It seems that he was spending too much time with the serving girl.'

'The folly of youth?'

'No, the folly of the serving girl. She misunderstood

the scope of her duties.'

'Ah!' Ludovica chortled with delight. 'Then we may shortly hear of another illegitimate offering—'

'Yes, indeed!'

'To match the son of Ser Piero!'

The women cackled. Annoyed by their banter Dante shuffled away, wandering through the shops and stalls. He eyed the racks of bream, the waxy onions, bulbs of garlic and knobs of gorgonzola, the *braccia* of dyed cloth and coils of bright silken thread, the dried leaves and sprigs of various herbs, those glossy red and green peppers that had become so popular. But he daydreamed as well, wondering if he might one day return to the stream and dare to swim—

'*Giovanotto*, good morning!'

Dante started. A woman was standing alongside him, inspecting the peppers. She was clear-eyed and elegant, and she was accompanied by a large man with a luxurious beard, a doublet threaded with the blue of the peacock and an expensive-looking cap.

The woman said, 'Husband, this is one of the young players from the village that I was telling you about.'

They nodded and shook hands. Dante introduced himself and the man spoke.

'I am Signor Alessandro de Torriano and this is my wife, Carlotta.'

De Torriano?

Alessandro said, 'I hear that I missed a—what is the

right word?—a remarkable performance. You were the creator?'

'No,' Dante told him, 'my friend Leo—'

Carlotta murmured to her husband. Alessandro laughed, too loudly.

'Ah, the famous monkey! Well, congratulations anyway. I am told that it was, for the most part, a great success.' He stepped aside and said, 'Annalisa, did you enjoy the performance?'

Dante realised the girl had been standing behind her parents the whole time. Not surprisingly, she looked more subdued than the last time he had seen her.

'I did, Father.'

'It's an exciting time in the *contado*, is it not?'

'Yes, it is.'

Alessandro laughed again and patted his daughter's cheek.

He said to Dante, 'Bellomo, you say? I have heard that name in passing. Your father is, perhaps, a member of the guild?'

'He is a saddle-maker, sir.'

'Ah, the minor guild, then. Still, that is the sign of a good man, hard-working no doubt. You must offer him my compliments. We might even do business one day? A secure saddle in exchange for a jar of fresh ginger, perhaps?'

Dante tilted his head. Alessandro seemed satisfied.

He glanced up and declared, 'The sun at its zenith

tells me that it is time for a cup of wine.'

'Perhaps,' said his wife, 'this well-mannered boy could show our daughter the rest of the marketplace?'

'An excellent idea!' Alessandro clapped Dante hard on the shoulder. 'Young Bellomo,' he said boisterously, 'son of a saddle-maker and monkey extraordinaire, I thank you for your kind offer.'

They sat on a stone ledge in a laneway beside the village's church. The vista was different here—an uncropped meadow surrounding the graveyard and the ossuary—and it was quieter, with only a pair of dogs and a snoozing peasant for company.

Annalisa told Dante about being disciplined for her excursion into the forest, then she smiled thinly and said, 'But you are safe enough, for my father seems to like you.'

'That is pleasing,' Dante told her, but he was thinking, *your father congratulated me on being a monkey. I don't care whether he likes me or not!*

Annalisa said slowly, 'I have an idea.'

He waited.

She tilted her face, sighed elaborately and said, 'My parents and my brothers are too busy to bother with me. Yet if I am to leave the villa and enjoy myself even the tiniest amount, then I must be chaperoned by someone whom my father knows and approves of.'

The dogs yapped softly as they rolled in the dust.

'Someone like you,' she added. 'He would allow that.'

His presence used as a way of granting her freedom; Dante was not so foolish as to believe that she craved his companionship. But was her true intention to get closer to Leo? His charismatic friend could certainly cast an enchanting spell.

His suspicions deepened when Annalisa murmured, 'Anyway, more of that later. Tell me about the King of the Forest.'

He shrugged, looking to the paler reaches of the sky.

'What do you want to know?'

'What did he mean when he spoke of having two mothers?'

'It is true, after a fashion,' Dante told her. He explained as best he could: Leo's birth mother, Catarina, had never married his father, but was now married to another and living elsewhere. His stepmother, Albiera, had recently passed away.

'Then he has two, but none.'

Dante nodded. Annalisa shook her head, as if to regulate the idea.

She said, 'Does he really want to be an artist? There are many more useful professions.'

'Leo could be anything,' Dante said defensively. 'The greatest stonemason or the greatest engineer or the greatest tanner; it wouldn't matter. Whatever he does, he will always be the greatest.'

'You admire your friend and I admire your loyalty. Is his art so worthwhile?'

'You saw the performance,' Dante reminded her. 'Leo constructed and painted the masks—'

'All of them?'

'In less than two days.' Dante shook his head. 'Once he has an idea—'

'Then he is determined?'

'More than anyone in the world, I am sure of it. And he loves to draw. If he sees a face that sparks his curiosity, he will follow that person for the whole day so that he may commit their image more truthfully to his page.'

Annalisa seemed to find this bemusing, but she said, 'Tell me more.'

So Dante related the story of a local villager who had asked Ser Piero if his son could decorate a plaque on his behalf.

'A commission?'

'Of sorts. The man was not wealthy. He simply wanted a gift for his family.' But Leo had painted an image of writhing, spitting snakes that was so terrifying, the villager refused to have the plaque back in his home.

Annalisa asked, 'Was Leo's father angry?'

Dante shook his head. 'No,' he said. 'Rather, Ser Piero saw an opportunity. He took the plaque to Florence and sold it to a dealer for more money than the villager was able to provide.'

'So, the dealer has it now?'

'No, again.' Dante grinned. 'Leo told me that the dealer has in turn sold the painting for a profit.'

'Making everyone happy, except the poor villager,' Annalisa said.

Dante chose not to comment. Such matters were a reflection of their world.

Annalisa's eyes were flickering.

She said, 'I wonder who owns it now?' and Dante told her that he had recently heard that the buyer was none other than the Duke of Milan.

She was suitably impressed, then gone shortly after, headed back to the villa with her parents and her two brothers: one blank-faced and silent, the other strapping and uproarious. But as Dante weaved through the stalls and shopfronts to find Ludovica, he wondered some more about Annalisa de Torriano. He thought that she was earnest and clever, and certainly witty with her words. If her father granted her permission, was it possible that their companionship could become a proper friendship?

Or more?

A whimsical idea: how would it be if he, the Not-So-Great Bellomo, fell in love with Annalisa, but she in turn was in love with his best friend, the Undeniably Great Leonardo? That would surely provide a plot worthy of the great Boccaccio.

Fruitless thinking. Dante knew that such an outcome was impossible because of the code that was never stated but always understood: boys like him were not worthy of girls like her. His job was to show her the *contado*, not to interfere with the arrangement of her no doubt glorious future.

When he reached the eastern side of the *piazza*, his grandmother was already on her feet, beady eyes scanning the crowd.

'Hurry up, dreamer, you're late! If I stay in this Godforsaken place any longer, I'll catch a chill and die, and it'll be your fault!'

Dante apologised and escorted her away. The farewell calls of Emilia and Dottorina followed him home, as if he had a cackling raven perched on each shoulder.

CHAPTER 9

Awakening

Messages were delivered and the idea was cautiously outlined. Raised eyebrows were followed by a closed door and an agonising period of deliberation. When the door creaked open, a final answer was delayed until instructions could be issued and warnings checked for understanding. Thereafter—

Permission was granted!

Dante arrived before the specified time. Annalisa, peeking around the edge of an arras, spotted him waiting in front of the villa and was surprised to realise how small and frail-looking he was. He had the lightness of a baby bird, the trepidation too. As he stood near the statue that dominated the forecourt—Ceres, casting her motherly eyes over crop and tree—Dante might have been peering out of a nest, getting nervous about the process of flying and landing.

Briefly, she wondered, *how and where would the winds*

take such a being?

For all that, he had been approved as her companion, meaning that as well as escorting her, he would have the pleasure of listening, no doubt with great courtesy and interest, to her diverse and, of course, substantial opinions.

She went outside. Having greeted each other cordially and touched Ceres on the foot for good luck, they took a path that meandered through scrolls of pampas grass made crisp and lemony by the sun, and travelled past the southern end of the village, towards the river. Although it was only mid-morning, the day was already heavy, the skin of the sky beginning to darken and crack as if wearied by age.

Annalisa was listing her flotilla of Florentine friends for no other purpose than Dante's envy when she saw Luca on horseback, cantering towards them. As always, her brother's broad smile suggested that he was alive to any possibility.

'Anna?' he called. 'What's this? Are you and this daring young fox eloping?'

Dante made a strange choking noise. Luca reined the horse to a halt as Annalisa shook her head at her brother's absurdity.

'No,' she said, 'although I *am* hoping to achieve my greatest desire.'

'Which is?'

'To get away from you, dear brother.'

'Impossible,' Luca told her, 'for like the stench of manure in this wretched hole, I am everywhere.' He waved a theatrical greeting in Dante's direction, then said to Annalisa, 'So, you are *exploring*?'

'Again, no. This is a day of education. I am being tutored in the benefits of country life.'

'Ah! The city's fairest maiden wishes to become one of the land's many mistresses. As your brother and mentor, I must urge you to be cautious.'

'Oh, must you? A week or two in the *contado* and you are now an expert?'

'I am a man; that provides expertise enough.'

Annalisa laughed. 'You may be a man,' she said, 'but out here, your hands are as soft as your heart. Be honest, brother, you are as misplaced as I.'

'Not at all. Anna, are you even aware of the pitfalls that lie around you? For example, did you know that if you stand for too long on this eager soil, roots will sprout from your feet and leaves from your arms? Soon enough, you will no longer be Annalisa de Torriano, bright star of Florence. Instead, you will become a wizened tree, condemned to remain throughout time in that one spot, to be wind-blown and rained upon, to have birds squawk and squat—and mess!—upon your head. The people of the future will stroll past and say, "That old thing? That is the Torriano Tree, a grim reminder of the perils of country living."'

'Go,' she said, mock-angry.

Luca grinned. 'I bid you farewell,' he said. 'All things considered, it has been a pleasure to have you as my sister.'

He jigged his heels and the horse rose into a gallop, like Pegasus winging to the unknown margins of the Earth.

They watched the dust settle, then Dante said in his understated way, 'Your brother is lively.'

'He drives us mad and we love him dearly for that.' Annalisa gathered the pleats in her dress. 'Shall we walk?'

But as she continued to regale Dante with details of her life in Florence, the contrast of those brilliant memories against her current situation led her into disappointment, and she began to wonder if she'd been too generous in her earlier assessments of the countryside. Looking around, she saw that the trees were more stunted than grand, the hills low and grey, the plains lifeless and empty. She hoped that the river would prove to be as exciting as the forest's cataract, but upon arrival, she found it to be sluggish, brown and unappealing. Trudging across the escarpment, Annalisa couldn't help but think that anyone hoping to paint such a world should reconsider, because the canvas would be unsellable, no matter the skill of the artist. Buyers would yawn and turn away, and soon enough the painting would be tossed into a cellar and forgotten.

Tired of wandering and dispirited with what had seemed, this morning, like such a good idea, an increasingly irritable Annalisa insisted that they rest in a shady hollow that overlooked the river. Dante agreed and they sat in stony silence, watching the dragonflies dance, until—

'O Great Bellomo!'

'Leo!' Dante struggled to his feet. 'Where did you come from?'

'Where else but the sky?' Leo, looking as fresh as if he'd just awoken, dropped the bag that he was carrying and proclaimed, 'An amazing event! This morning, I was kidnapped by a kite, but when I told the good fellow that I had an appointment with the Royal *Palazzo*, he agreed to bring me here.'

'You're lying!'

'No, it's true. Look, there is my kidnapper.'

They followed his gesture and saw that there was indeed a tawny kite, perched smugly on a branch that hung over the water.

Dante laughed happily.

He said, 'You were lucky that the kite was so understanding.'

'We are old adversaries,' grinned Leo, 'and therefore excellent friends. Have I not told you of my first experience with this bird? I was a baby, innocently cooing in my cradle, when the kite flew down, prised open my mouth with its tail and struck the insides of my lips.' He waved his hand back and forth across his face. 'Several strikes—*whap, whap!*

Annalisa was still irritable.

'Ridiculous,' she said. 'No bird would do such a thing. You must have dreamed that.'

'Signorina, you are here too! My apologies for missing a most significant presence, that of the Queen herself! Are you well?'

'Well enough, Your Majesty.'

'I am pleased to hear it, just as I am pleased to tell you about my adventures with my friend, the kite—'

'You mean, your dream.'

Leo considered.

'You're certain that I dreamed?'

'Of course I am. It's obvious.'

'You seem to be certain of many things.'

'Better that, than pointless dreaming.'

'Such pragmatism! Annalisa de Torriano, you are a true Florentine!'

'And what of it?'

'A statement of fact, nothing more. So, that is your final contention? I dreamed about the kite?'

'Of course. Who could believe otherwise?'

'Perhaps you are right,' said Leo. 'And yet, there is a moment at the point of awakening when every dream *seems* real and all of the emotions that are attached to it also seem real. So, it is difficult for us to know what is truth and what is not. Do you not agree?'

The idea was too bewitching; Annalisa couldn't reply. She felt the light shift and the river quieten, as if they were caught, suddenly, in a flux where nothing could move or prosper.

Heat and stillness, in thickening layers. She watched as Leo dropped to his haunches, opened his bag and tipped it upside-down.

'Look,' he said.

An object slid to the ground. Annalisa gasped at both the sight and the stench. The eyes of the dead squirrel were stones. Its tail was stiff with dirt and a crust of blood had settled around its mouth. Worst of all, the squirrel's claws were curled towards action, as if, in its final moments, the poor creature had tried to scurry away from its fate.

'This is no dream,' said Leo. He picked up the squirrel and rotated it in his hands, scrutinising each part of its anatomy. When Annalisa had recovered herself, he told her that he often collected dead animals.

Aghast, she asked, 'But why?'

'Because they interest me,' he said. 'Also, I have been asked to paint a fire-breathing monster onto a shield. The customer demands that it be as realistic as possible, however fire-breathing monsters are hard to locate at this time of the year and even harder to capture if you do happen to find one. As an alternative, I have been collecting dead animals so that I may distort their features in my art. This squirrel is my most recent acquisition. I found it this morning, beneath a tree.'

'But how may this poor deceased creature be turned

into a monster?'

'*Parts* of a monster,' Leo told her. 'I will borrow the lifelessness of the eyes and the stretch of the mouth.' He admired the squirrel for a moment longer, then dropped it back into the bag. 'Now,' he said, 'shall we go down to the water, before the storm comes?'

They did so, sitting on the riverbank as Leo sketched the scene into his notebook. Annalisa was surprised to see that he drew in reverse, with the wrong hand. When she asked him why, he said that his left hand had demanded to be used today.

'They squabble,' he told her. 'Tomorrow, the other might win.'

The sketching continued, along with a commentary about making the river more inviting and the sky more forbidding.

'I do this,' he explained, 'because an artist is the lord of all that he sees.'

Annalisa sniffed loudly.

'How pompous you are,' she said.

Undaunted, Leo continued.

'If the artist wishes to change the world by reimagining and perhaps improving its form, then he should do so. That is his right.'

When he had finished, he tore out the sketch and asked Annalisa to accept it as a gift. She was sceptical until she looked at the paper in her hand and saw, immediately, that the image was a triumph. The water seemed to ripple and the leaves shivered, and she was amazed how easily he had drawn the river as a connecting line between the indistinct end of the earth and the outlined shapes of three people who stood within the foreground; Leo, Dante and herself, she realised.

The lord of all that he sees.

Later that day, a storm did arrive. Annalisa rested on her bed as lightning spiked the land and a deluge blocked out the wider world. She wondered if the river might overflow and drown the lower tracts of the valley, then she reached beneath her pillow where she had hidden the sketch. Looking at it one more time, she found the delicacy of each backward chalk-mark to be warming, not unlike a smile. She traced the flow of the river with her fingertip and held the sketch close, hoping that it might tip her gently towards sleep.

CHAPTER 10

Seeking and Knowing

What he had felt in his own special way, the girl could now feel. Dante sensed that she too had been touched by the magic. That touch was light, like a moth landing on the brow of a sleeping child, but its mark was forever. After the undiscovered moth had flown back to the darkness, the silver dust that drifted from its wings would remain as a blessing, making the skin of the child glisten in a way that it never had before.

Allowing the child to awaken to a new world.

When I am with Leo, he thought, *I am shown the world in ways that I never could have imagined. The leaf of the oak is no longer merely a leaf, but a spine with diagonal ribs, each of which finishes with a sharp point . . .*

'Dante, like the feet of a waterbird!'

Summer clouds are feathery lines that become a hundred or more perfectly stacked eyelashes. The spider's web is a single shape repeated in links that create a perfect orb.

The seeds of the sunflower gather in the same spiral pattern as the scales on the pine cone. A woodpecker battering a tree is not just a bird building its nest but is a model for a machine . . .

'That such a tiny bird may force a hole through the toughness of bark is miraculous, Dante! Should we not study the structure of its head and neck, to see how the woodpecker finds its strength? Then we might build a machine with a similar structure, a machine that could break walls and destroy castles!'

'Why do we want to break walls and destroy castles?'

'My dear friend, *we* don't. But it would be interesting to know how to do so, should ever the need arise.'

Over time, Dante had learned that, for Leo, their planet was more than soil, rock and water, more than this entity that could be conveniently explained as God's creation. Earth was a giant mass of marvels that Leo needed to understand, and problems that he needed to solve. This was why it was commonplace for him to stop, point and blurt out questions.

'Dante, look. Why is that side of the hill shallow when the other side is steep?'

'I don't know.'

'Me neither, but there is a reason, just as there is a reason for the river breaking left at that particular point and not further downstream.'

'I suppose so.'

'Be curious, my dear friend! Fill yourself with wonder!

Now, something else. Assuming that they receive similar quantities of rainfall and sunshine, why are the crops on Signor Mancini's field more handsome than the crops on Signor Fanucci's field?'

'Perhaps Signor Mancini treats his crops with greater favour?'

'What, does he woo them with love songs? Baptise them and treat them as his children?'

'Of course not!'

'Dante, Mancini and Fanucci are partners, not rivals. They work together. Therefore, why the difference?'

So many questions! Leo's desire for knowledge was a deep, unquenchable thirst.

'Dante, look at that group of people over there.'

'Why?'

'Because they are *interesting!* Now, watch them speaking with each other. Do their lips move in the same way?'

'I don't know. I will never know.'

'But—'

'Leo, I am not like you. I will be forever ignorant.'

'Why so glum, Dante? No-one who is prepared to properly examine the world can be "forever ignorant". Raise yourself, my friend! Become the new sun! Now, see how the lady with the purple gown lifts her eyebrows? Does she do so deliberately, do you think, or is the action automatic, like blinking? Speaking of which, why do we blink? And why is that blinking sometimes fast and sometimes not?'

'I suppose there are reasons—'

'Of course! There are reasons for everything. Everything!'

More questions, an unending stream. What causes water to emerge from the inside of mountains? Why are there valleys? Has the world always been shaped the same? What makes the moon gleam? Why do snails shrivel to the touch? Why is the crocodile's jaw so long?

'I've never seen a crocodile.'

'Well, when you do, watch out for its jaw!'

What causes water to swirl in a vortex? Where does wind begin? What makes the sky blue?'

His was a world that was always in close-up, always demanding examination and explanation. For Dante, to be close to such grand thinking could be daunting, but he also saw it as a privilege that went beyond his entitlement or expectation. *And now*, he thought, *it seemed likely that confident, forthright Annalisa de Torriano of Florence—both different from* and *indifferent to his shy self—had been given the honour of sharing that rare privilege.*

They met on the side of one of the tracks that linked the village with the hills. Despite the early heat, Leo was wearing a short cloak in the colour of the hollyhock, making him look like a splash of dawn against the paleness of the morning fields. He was staring, apparently mesmerised.

Annalisa called, 'Hello!'

'Sshh!' He motioned for them to remain still.

Annalisa clicked her tongue and said to Dante, 'What's he doing?'

'I don't know. Praying?'

'Do you really think so? This collector of dead animals is given to spontaneous prayer?'

'Perhaps,' said Dante, 'he is observing. He likes to observe—'

'As do I, but observation is not normally an activity that requires silence.' Ignoring Leo's upheld hand, she called his name and moved forward.

'Oohh!' Leo waved his arms in exasperation, then turned to Annalisa. 'They're gone! You disturbed them!'

'Who? I saw no-one.'

'The bees!' Dante could hear the nettle in Leo's voice. 'I was watching them hover over these poppies!'

'Why would you bother to watch bees?'

'Because I am interested in the mechanics of flight,' Leo told her, as if this was the most standard curiosity in the world.

'And what did you discover, King of the Forest, before I so rudely interrupted you?'

Despite his annoyance, Leo could not prevent himself from smiling.

'It was fascinating,' he said. 'If you examine a dead bee, as I have done, you will see that the insect has four wings, two on either side. However, when the bee is alive and flying, these four wings suddenly become two.'

'Is such a feat even possible, or is this another of your hefty imaginations?'

'It is possible, because the bee joins his wings together.' Leo looked at Dante and said, 'O Great Bellomo, your arms, please.'

'My arms?'

'Yes! Come on!'

He made Dante stand in front of him and raise his arms in a V-shape, then stood close and replicated Dante's arms with his own, before gripping his friend's wrists.

'When I pull down, you do the same. Down, then up, repeat, repeat. You see how it goes? Four wings become two yet they still generate the same amount of power as four.'

They performed the manoeuvre several times, Dante feeling that his arms might be ripped out by Leo's strength of purpose. Annalisa's face betrayed her bemusement.

'You are still here,' she said. 'I expected you both to be flying over the clouds by now.'

'That was a demonstration of the science,' Leo told her. 'Nevertheless, it is true. One day, I would like to fly.'

This time, she laughed aloud.

'The King will become a bee?'

'No, I—'

'Then perhaps you will be a bird, a long-legged gull dragging his pink cloak across the sky!'

'No,' said Leo, suddenly very serious. 'I will remain a human, as has been ordained, however I will fly.'

Annalisa asked, 'Is it not enough for you to walk and run, like everyone else?'

'Walking and running are useful,' Leo agreed. 'So, too, riding and swimming. But I would like to fly.'

'Why?'

'Need you ask? To better see the world.'

'It seems to me,' said Annalisa wryly, 'that you already see the world well enough.'

'There is always more.' Leo stooped, plucked a poppy and placed it easily behind his ear. He said, 'Why be on Earth, if not to be curious? Why else be here?'

They were quiet until Dante surprised them by saying, 'Perhaps we are caretakers.'

'Meaning?'

'God has put us here to look after His works,' said Dante cautiously. 'We are like nurses to God's children.'

'You see how noble he is?' Leo's hug was impulsive, powerful. 'O wonderful, kind-hearted human; you must live forever! You must! We can all prosper from your immortality. Every creature will sing, every tree will applaud and every drop in the ocean will whisper its contentment! There will be festivals in every town in every country and the people will proclaim: "The Great

Bellomo is here and all is well with the world!"'

After which came what they would later call The Day of The Birds, Leo telling them that just as fish must swim to stay alive, creatures which were designed for flight should be allowed to fly, whereas in the village there were birds in cages, awaiting sale.

'What's wrong with that?' asked Annalisa. 'In Florence, there are bird-sellers on every street corner.'

'Would you like to be imprisoned in a cage?' Leo countered. 'Would you like to be separated from your family, and stared at and treated like a curiosity?'

The plan was simple. Annalisa would approach the seller and express interest in buying a bird—'The one in the furthest corner,' Leo instructed. While the seller was negotiating a price, Leo would unhook the doors of the other cages and release the songbirds, siskins, linnets and goldfinches—'Each one, no matter their species. No bird is of greater importance than any other. No creature is of greater importance than any other. All rank equally,' he lectured.

'Below humans,' said Annalisa quickly.

'No, the same as humans. We are creatures too.'

'We are surely better than creatures!' Her tone verged on indignation.

'No, we are the same. Creatures have skin, bone, muscles and organs, as well as a system for the movement of the blood, and a system for thinking. So do we.'

'No, we are different, very different! We are better!'

'How so?'

'Well,' she said, 'we don't just have "a system for thinking", we have a proper intelligence—'

'Creatures have intelligence—'

'For their own survival,' Annalisa insisted, 'whereas our intelligence shapes the world!'

Leo said quickly, firmly, 'Your comment presumes a greater significance for human thought and endeavour. I simply ask: can you or I spin a web? Can we swim underwater without the need for breath? More to the point, can we fly?'

A brief silence until Dante said, 'What will I do?'

Leo turned.

'Do?'

'While you are freeing the birds?'

'What you always do, O Valorous Warrior—keep watch! Yell out if any overly responsible citizens or murderous members of the military happen to trot by.'

They went to work. Six birds were gone, flitting over the rooftops, before the seller realised. Dante and Annalisa rushed away, but Leo did not move. Cowering in the churchyard, Dante risked a glance and saw his friend calmly handing over several coins while the bird-seller continued to complain and threaten.

'He brought money,' Annalisa whispered. 'He knew all along what he was going to do.'

Dante could not tell whether she spoke in anger or admiration.

It was the following day, sitting together in a field without Annalisa perched between them, when Dante plucked up the courage to ask, 'Are we now three?'

Leo considered.

'Others may join the Royal *Palazzo*,' he said, 'but the original bond will always be the strongest.'

'Really?'

'Oh, yes.' He put down his chalk and notebook, and gripped Dante's hand. 'You and I are heart and soul,' he said. 'Nothing can separate those.'

CHAPTER 11

Mystery

With her father briefly back in the city to plot with friends and undermine enemies—or was it the other way around?—her brothers giving orders and riding across the paddocks, and her mother immersed in a whirl of social events, Annalisa's summer took on a greater freedom than she had previously known. The strict patterns and expectations of city life now seemed remote as she continued to explore the countryside, all the time listening to Leo, challenging him, jousting with him . . .

Becoming more and more amazed by him.

And something else: Matteo Piombino, she realised one fine morning, was now an indifferent memory, of no more consequence than idly recalling an unremarkable meal.

Sometimes, instead of their daily ramblings, the members of the Royal *Palazzo* of the Forest met at court, at the cataract, which Annalisa began to relish as a place of great beauty and tranquillity. It was here, one warm and dimpled afternoon, that Leo surprised her, although not Dante, with his latest plan for adventure.

'There is a cave,' he said.

He was lolling on a throne of moss-covered rock with his bare feet diverting the flow of the water. Annalisa, sitting close enough to be included in the conversation but sufficiently apart to maintain her self-respect, was struck, once again, by his unique appearance: long, tapering nose, lips that never stilled—Leo would chatter in his sleep!—and those eyes that changed colour, she imagined, in synchrony with the seasons: green eyes in spring; brightly cornflower blue as they were now in summer; a gentler brown in autumn; grey and perhaps more judgmental in winter.

'This again,' said Dante. He was seated even further away on a fallen tree.

Leo looked across. 'You do not believe that I can do it?'

'Do what?' asked Annalisa.

'There is a cave,' said Leo again, as he withdrew his feet from the water and inspected his toes. 'I discovered it some time ago, but, as yet, I have not been inside.'

'So?' Annalisa yawned. The velvety air was making her sleepy.

'So, I want to see what lies within.'

'Then why didn't you look when you discovered this cave?'

'Because I was scared,' Leo told her, in the same tone

that he might have admitted to being hungry or tired.

Annalisa stared at him.

'I can't imagine you ever being scared,' she said.

'Well, I was.' Leo flexed his wrists. 'Like anyone who treads into the unknown, I am excited by the idea of discovery but also worried about what I might find. Still, our fears must be set aside if the ocean is to be crossed or the mountain climbed. Or, in this case, the cave entered and explored.'

'Is that what you are doing? Setting your fears aside?'

Leo didn't answer. Instead, as they departed the Royal Court, he outlined his plan. The cave was in a deeper section of the forest, located near the base of a rocky rise and protected by spiky weeds and vines. Get through that layer and the entrance was narrow but surely worth the effort, Leo being certain that the cave's interior would herald a spectacular vista of rock formations.

'And beasts?'

'Possibly. Bears are said to live in caves.'

'As are bats—'

'And many other creatures: dragons, demons, tribes of Gorgades, perhaps even the mighty Minotaur. Two Minotaurs! Anyway, we will find out soon enough.'

'We?' said Annalisa.

Leo nodded. They were back in the meadow where the sun beat down and the smell of harvestable crops was pungent. Annalisa felt alive with daring.

'Very well,' she told him. 'Tomorrow.'

'Excellent. Dante? You'll be there, won't you?'

The smaller boy, who'd been quiet all afternoon, nodded his agreement.

The next day was hotter than any she had previously experienced, the midsummer sky trapping the air beneath an overlay of polished glass. The Royal Palazzo met behind the Torriano chapel and approached the forest from a different, northerly aspect, so as to shorten the journey to the cave. Annalisa soon saw that, in here, nature had inverted. The creepers were muscular, like Luca's forearms, and the trees were misshapen, as if formed from nature's leftovers. As she trod into the gloom, each pocket of mystery behind the cuts and angles of green seemed to fill with strange whirs and buzzes. The scuttling from the forest floor gave her a sense of being spied on by unknown beings making pronouncements with their unearthly voices: 'Look at them, come from another world . . . follow them closely for they do not belong.'

It was a relief, then, to leave the track, scramble up a shallow incline and reach the tapestry of olive and charcoal that Leo identified as concealing the entrance to the cave. They stood in awkward contemplation, until Dante said, 'I will wait here.'

Leo turned.

'Dante, no! This will be a sight to behold! It will be

more divine than the frescoes of Fra Angelico, more beautiful than Masaccio's Garden! Such wonders must be seen by all of us!'

Annalisa noticed an uncharacteristic hardening in Dante's pretty eyes, in the set of his mouth.

'No,' he said. 'I will keep watch. I always keep watch, remember?'

'Yes, but—'

'You two do what you must and I will wait here.'

Leo sighed.

'Very well,' he said. Without waiting any longer, he dived into the vines, flexing and thrashing before he re-emerged like a swimmer and used his elbows to forge an opening.

'Come,' he said to Annalisa. 'The Minotaurs await.'

Determined to appear brave, she followed him, taking care not to scratch herself as she did so. At the thin entrance to the cave, plants hung from a lip of moss like cobwebs. The effect was eerie, making the *loggia*, with its sunny views, pots of flowers and smells of roasting meats wafting from the kitchen, seem very inviting.

What lay within? A light ripple of fear passed through her—but Leo had already entered the cave, his voice echoing as he called, 'No bears—not yet, anyway!'

Annalisa whispered a prayer and made the Sign before hitching her dress and shuffling through the entrance. A moment for her eyes to adjust to the absence of light . . .

Shapes.

The stink of old soil.

Movement? No, but a faint dripping sound.

She fought against disorientation. To her right lay a blank wall of rock. Further on, a weak glow offset the blackness.

'There is a fissure,' said Leo. She could just see his outline, against the wall. 'A crack in the earth's surface,' he explained, 'where the light gets in.'

Despite this, he sounded disappointed and she knew why. Even with limited vision, she could see that the cave was uninspiring. During their trek through the forest, Leo had been vocal about his expectations: a subterranean joy filled with awe-inspiring drops and elevations. But this cave seemed minor, little more than a dent.

She watched his hands brushing across the rock as if he was checking its properties, then she said, 'Time to go.' There was little point in staying. The cave offered nothing and besides, there would be other areas to explore—

'Wait.' He'd stopped where the light feathered the wall and was continuing to scan with his long fingers.

'But it's dull,' she complained, knowing that the accusation would hurt him. *Dull and cramped*, she thought, *and dirty and smelly, and certainly not the place for a Florentine girl of my standing.*

'A moment more.' He took a small step back, studied something that she couldn't see, then reached out and slowly traced along the wall with both hands.

'Yes,' he said. 'Oh yes, I think so!'

Annalisa squinted at the area where he was tracing. Nothing but rock.

'This is a find,' he said, 'a great find!'

'Leo? I cannot see—'

He told her in hushed tones: here was a fossil. Millions of years ago, an animal had died in this place and been buried in mud. Over time, the mud had hardened into rock, reforming the precise shape of the animal's bones.

'A fossil?'

'Yes.'

'Here?'

'Yes!'

'You are touching the remains of an animal from *that* long ago?' For Annalisa, the scale of the idea was incredible. *Millions* of years! She shivered, as the thrill of history enfolded them.

'The fossilised remains,' he agreed. 'The size and shape suggest that these are the teeth of a giant animal—possibly even a whale.'

The dripping, the thin pipe of light. Oddly, although she was inside the planet, Annalisa felt removed from its solidity.

Her voice trembled as she asked, 'But how might a whale, a creature which lives in the deepest sea, enter a mountain cave?'

'It can only have been,' said Leo, 'that this was not always a cave. If, by some accident of nature, we fell asleep and woke up in the most distant past, it may be that we would find ourselves underwater, in the bed of a great ocean.'

Annalisa shook her head. Surely not! God had created the world as it was now. The only changes were those engineered by people: the roads and farms, the great cities. Not what he was suggesting, this . . .

Enormity. An alteration so vast, it was impossible for her to conceive.

'The whale is a mighty creature.' Leo's voice seemed to travel through the semi-light as a separated being. 'Perhaps the mightiest, and yet . . .'

She whispered, 'What are you saying?'

'That might does not matter,' he told her. 'Strength, or power, or the form in which you are created: none of these things matter. We are the whale and the whale is us. Like all creatures, we come and we go. We may have our differences, but we are united.'

'United—how?'

His answer was whispered, each word creating its own tiny echo.

'By the gift of life and the certainty of death,' he said.

Nothing more, for either of them. Annalisa was grateful when Leo stepped towards her and gently suggested that now was the right time to return to the daylight.

'We will leave our friend, the whale, in peace,' he said. 'He has earned that right.'

CHAPTER 12

Death and Departure

He was disturbed by a hand on his shoulder, then a voice spinning through the darkness like a broken-winged bird.

'Dante, beloved son—oh, Dante!'

There had been no warning. Ludovica had eaten well, complained about the meal as she always did, reminded them that the Devil's reach was long and his grip fierce, and retired with the sun. Early the next morning, her distraught maid had been unable to wake her.

'Fifty-eight!' said Dante's mother, Amara, tearfully. 'That we all should live to such an age!'

Stefano Bellomo did not respond. His face was mottled, unhealthy-looking. He swigged from a stone jar before saying to Dante, 'Boy, go and take a final look at your grandmother before the nurse does what she must.'

Dante went reluctantly. The air inside the room was

uncomfortably warm. In death, Ludovica looked much as she had in life: thin and hard, angular, peevish. Dante stood at the end of her bed and wondered if she might rise unannounced, wave a bony finger and admonish him for being lazy when he could be running after the goats or organising a trip to the village for her. A silly notion, ridiculous—but when he knelt to offer her a prayer, he realised that he was crying and the tears would not cease when he wanted them to, and he wished that Leo was there, with him, because Leo would make sense of this, as only Leo could.

Long days, longer nights. His grandmother was washed and wrapped. Amara insisted on herbs to beautify the body and the old woman's favoured icon was bound tightly into her cold hands. Dante, hoping for a sweep of new stars to break open the sky, overheard a disagreement.

'Amara, I have made the arrangements. My mother will be buried in the graveyard.'

'Husband, please! Why not the church? Ludovica deserves—'

'She is getting exactly what she deserves.'

'Can you not be more generous?'

'The graveyard is good enough. Besides, we cannot afford the church.'

'We, who own this land and more, cannot inter your mother in a church?'

'Woman, enough. I have made my decision.'

'But, Stefano—'

'Oh, stop your carping! Already, you are beginning to sound like her. I am rid of one shrew and straightaway another takes her place!'

'Stefano!'

'The graveyard it is.'

Sniffling, like the mewling of a lost cat. His father's voice relented, but only a little.

'Amara, it doesn't matter; none of this matters. My mother is dead and she'll be put in the ground. That's all there is.'

Another morning without light. In the village, a bell rang. Dante trooped behind the cart and his father's lame, irregular step. The bell kept ringing, and Dante wondered if God had decreed that those peals should never end, that their clanging madness should provide the dirge that would usher Ludovica into eternity.

The congregation assembled and the priest intoned standard rites. Dante's grandmother was clad in a cheese-coloured gown that seemed to blend with her pallor, turning her into a nameless, featureless object. Quickly, precisely, she was lowered into the clay. Dante rubbed his eyes. When his vision cleared, he saw Leo standing with his Uncle Francesco and Aunt Violante and he felt, across the air, a warm, salty rush, not unlike the breaking of the sea.

The meal afterwards was necessarily limited. Dottorina wailed. Emilia, who had been calm throughout, decided to join her. At nightfall, after they had departed and the family had retired, the house felt empty and dusty. *No, worse*, thought Dante. *It felt bloodless.*

They slept and awoke, ate and drank, worked, adjusted their ways. His father spent longer than usual attending to his saddle-making business. His mother closed doors so that she might weep alone before emerging, pale-faced, to organise the household. Dante was told to stay at home and deal with the cows and the goats, the scrabbling chickens. He was aware of more conversations between his parents, but these were private whisperings, not for his ears.

One morning he saw Leo standing in the adjoining field, wrapped in his rose-coloured cloak and looking like a resplendent scarecrow. Dante ran towards him.

'Dear friend!'

They embraced. Released from the cloak, Leo's arms felt smooth and strong. The beginnings of a beard lined his chin and jaw.

Dante said, 'I am to remain with my parents—'

'For a time.' They stepped back. Leo's smile was cautious but warm. 'O Great Bellomo,' he said kindly, 'we miss you at the Royal *Palazzo.*'

Dante felt a sharpness in his spine.

'Then you still meet?'

'No,' said Leo, touching Dante's hand. 'No, we do not meet, but we do miss you.'

Comforting, he thought, and what he needed to hear, for it was unsettling, the extent to which he lamented the death of his grandmother. A cantankerous crone, miserable and bitter, slanderous and selfish, yet he continued to yearn for her difficult presence.

Ten days after burying his mother, Stefano Bellomo returned from a brief trip to Florence, limped into the villa, removed his boots, drew a cup of beer and said, 'Wife, boy, come here and stand before me.'

Dante followed his mother. They stood side-by-side as Stefano outlined his scheme in a voice that was as coarse as the rasps that he used to shape the pommels and cantles.

'We shall not stay,' he said.

He was selling the house and moving the family back to Florence, permanently.

'It is a sham.' He glared at the walls, as if they might challenge him. 'Are we here because of our love for the *contado*? Because we are loyal to this rustic village and life? No, we are here because we stoop to the petty prejudices of those in the major guilds. Wife, do you know what they think?'

'Stefano, I cannot—'

'That your hard-working husband does not count, for he is *merely* a saddle-maker! Oh, publicly they agree that such jobs are necessary, but privately there is always a whisper; that our trade is limited, that we saddle-makers are not especially skilled. Naturally we must defer to those who are; we must defer to the *popolo*! Yes, we who are *mere* must bow to the judges and bankers and moneychangers, and those nose-up men of silk and wool and fur and spices, men like that pompous fool Alessandro de Torriano, who paid a trifling price for the Poggio villa after poor old Emanuele was declared bankrupt by those heartless curs! Well, it is ridiculous, and I, for one, won't be playing those games anymore! The Bellomos belong in Florence with the rest of them. We have always belonged in Florence.'

'But the expense?' Amara's face was pale.

'Expense!' Stefano spat the word onto the flagstones. 'What does that matter? I'm a decent man with a decent—and skilled!—profession. I have every right to live in the greatest city in the world and that's what I'm going to do.'

His father's edict made Dante miserable. *I have one true friend*, he thought, *one—and now this! Stuck in busy, bewildering Florence, never to see Leo again—*

Stefano turned to him and said gruffly, 'Boy, it's time for you to grow up. There's more to life than wandering the meadows like a lost donkey and putting on pagan shows with that misfit friend of yours.'

'The son of Ser Piero is said to possess an extraordinary intelligence,' said Amara.

'I don't care if he's smarter than Socrates, anyone born to a fool's mistress will always be a misfit.' Stefano hawked, then indicated that Dante should sit beside him. He hesitated, only moving when his mother's hands guided him.

More throat-clearing. Dante cringed. His father smelled of rawhide and horsehair, and there was sawdust trapped like tiny spores in the hair on his arms.

'Boy,' he said, 'to be idle is the domain of the very young and the privilege of the very old. In between those ages, we work. Now, heed my instruction.'

The second part of the plan: once the family had returned to the city, Dante would learn how to be a soldier and, in time, join the Florentine infantry.

No!

Stefano said, 'My uncle's friend, Gaspare di Loreto, was a fine soldier, a survivor of Anghiari and skilled enough to be drafted into the defence of none other than the late, great Cosimo Medici. He now runs a school for those who wish to learn the noble art of warfare. Dante, I have made inquiries. You will attend this school forthwith.'

He looked for his mother and realised that she had slipped out of the room. His father grasped his arm.

'The Bellomos have long been soldiers,' said Stefano, 'until this stupid leg of mine came along. Now we will be soldiers again and the arrogant *popolo* can see our mettle for exactly what it is.'

'Father, I—'

'What, boy? Spit it out!'

But the words refused to come. Stefano strengthened his hold on Dante's arm.

'Listen to me,' he hissed. 'Our family does not need another bow-backed saddle-maker, hacking his fingers to the bone. Yes, there is money, and yes, there is constancy, but what of glory? What of the history of our name? I tell you, Dante, it is time for the Bellomos to rise again, rise like we did at San Romano, like we did forty years ago against those upstarts from Milan!'

'Please, Father, my arm!'

Stefano, looking down, realised the power of his grip.

He released Dante before adding, 'Make no mistake, warfare brings prestige. Reminding the arrogant Milanese and those idiots from Pisa of their true place in the world brings prestige, as well as riches and substance. We can have all the bankers and lawyers, architects and wool-sellers—and saddle-makers—that we like, but it is men of war who forge the future! This is the life that I want for you, my only son.'

He used his fingers to turn Dante's face towards his own.

'You will live in the tradition of the *nonno* whom you never knew,' he insisted. 'And you will progress. This, I know. You will learn to ride and fight, then the day will come when you are no longer a soft-hatted member of the infantry but part of the *feditore*, the cavalry strike force. When that happens, as it inevitably will, you will ride out at the forefront of the army and defend our city, defend our way of life. What an honour for our family! What glory!'

Don't cry, he thought. *Not now. Don't.*

His father took away his fingers and spat hard onto the floor.

He said, 'Dante, if I have learned one thing about life, it is this: better to sit high in the saddle than to be forced into making the damned thing.'

CHAPTER 13

Corruptions

Annalisa had heard about the death of Dante's grandmother and was mildly concerned on his behalf, however, her greater worry was that, without her approved companion in tow, she had been unable to legitimately leave the villa and see Leo. Late one morning, bored and grumpy, she decided that whatever the consequence, she must find a way. Perhaps a firmly closed door and something more for Martina, who was already being provided with an extra *soldo* for quietly cleaning and fixing Annalisa's tatty clothes.

But before she could put her plan into action, Annalisa was summoned into the *loggia*, where her father, who had returned from Florence late the previous evening, and her mother were formally posed, as if for a portrait-sitting.

'Dear child!' said Alessandro, with what seemed, for him, an over-supply of affection.

'*Buongiorno*, Father, Mother.'

'Anna, I have good news.'

'Wonderful news!' Her mother's words piped like notes from a hautboy and her face glowed through the thick, white powder that she applied every morning.

Having decided to play the dutiful daughter, Annalisa stood patiently as her father arose and stroked her cheek. *As if I were a child*, she thought, *a child once more* . . . When she was little, he had always stroked her cheek. And then, inexplicably, he hadn't.

'Anna, here it is. You are to be married!'

'Heavens be praised!' Carlotta was also off her seat, pulling her daughter into a fierce hug and kiss. 'Do you hear your father, sweet one? Married!'

Annalisa swayed. She felt light-headed, unable to breathe—

Her mother stepped back and clapped her hands triumphantly.

'My only daughter, a bride!'

Annalisa's voice emerged as a croak. 'Father, to whom?'

'A young man from a most reputable Florentine family,' said Alessandro proudly. 'The Piombinos have considerable wealth and land holdings, and Matteo, their eldest son, is astute of mind and devout of heart.'

'A very attractive match,' said Carlotta. Her eyes were gleaming.

'Oh, yes,' agreed her husband. He gripped Annalisa by the shoulders and assessed her as a critic might do with a new artwork. 'Matteo Piombino,' he said. 'Worthy, and worth plenty. You know how it goes, *piccolina*. You will soon grow to love him.'

She was given leave to return to her room and contemplate her new status. When she paused in the doorway, her parents' voices continued to echo through the villa.

'Alessandro, of course she is overwhelmed! But, husband, with happiness! I felt the same way when my own betrothal was announced.'

'Whereas for me, it was relief. A man needs a wife if he is to properly progress in this world. Stay unmarried, and they look at you with suspicion. Soon after, the whispering begins . . . no wife means no money, a bad catch.'

'You were relieved,' said Carlotta, 'and I was filled with a bliss that I had never known before, nor even imagined possible.'

'How so?'

'My dear husband, for a woman, marriage gives purpose—and the prospect of children! It fills every conceivable space in our lives. Of course I was happy!'

Annalisa closed her door. Through the window of her bedroom: the fruity aromas of summer, the calls of farmers and the muted responses of their animals, pastels shimmering and bleeding. In the distance, the whisperings of the forest. And somewhere within, the silent majesty of an ancient whale, sole resident of a cave.

Breathe, she thought. Once, then again. *Breathe*.

Suddenly, without knowing how it had happened, she was into the bright noon sunshine and careening towards the river.

He was standing before the water, head bowed, writing in his notebook. She called his name, but Leo remained where he was, telling her to, 'Look! Look!'

Annalisa stood beside him. She watched the river deflecting indigo and silver into the heart of the sky, then she said, too abruptly, 'What are you doing?'

He'd been sent by his Uncle Francesco to catch some fish.

'But I struggle,' he said, 'for unless I wish to properly examine the animal, it distresses me to see a trout on a string, trying in vain to enjoy its life and avoid being eaten by humans.'

Instead, he had brought apple cores.

'Why?' she asked.

'Because they float.' He pointed towards the water. 'That one—A—is close by and his friend B is nearer the centre. I have been measuring their progress as they navigate the river. I threw them in at the same time, in parallel, but see how B is further downstream? That means the current is stronger and more direct along the spine of the river. Here, in the shallow water near the bank, poor little A meanders.'

Annalisa shook her head.

'How is that even interesting?' she asked.

When he looked at her, she was, once again, transfixed by his eyes, those deep wells of knowledge and curiosity.

'Something bothers you,' he said.

'How can you know that?'

'Your manner,' Leo told her. 'Your colour.'

'My colour is—'

'Your blood runs fast,' he said.

Annalisa bit her lip.

'I must marry.' Her skin felt overly warm, and she had the beginnings of a headache. 'Oh, he is well-born and I am told that satisfies all requirements, and I believe his nature is pleasant enough—well, as pleasant as any man's nature *can* be, however, despite all of that, despite . . .'

'You do not care for marriage?'

'I do not care for marriage *now*,' Annalisa corrected. How quickly her life had altered! She waited for some show of empathy, but Leo simply nodded and reopened his notebook.

'Well?' she said indignantly. 'You say nothing. Are you suddenly without a voice?'

'I have a voice.'

'Then will you use it, or, God forbid, do you have no opinion for once?'

Leo was scribbling as he said, 'I was considering the

better fortune that exists in our world for those born as males.'

'What is the point of thinking that?' Annalisa glowered. 'I cannot change that!'

'No,' he agreed, 'you cannot. Anyway, Florence has rules.'

'Do you mean laws? There is no law stating that I must marry Matteo Piombino.'

'Is that his name? Very ornate. Not a law, no, but there are rules of conduct that hold us more firmly than any law.'

'You're saying I should just accept this?'

'I cannot tell you what to do or not to do,' said Leo. He lowered his notebook. 'I simply note that in Florence, it is easier—and safer—to challenge a natural law than it is to challenge a man-made rule—'

'How does that matter!'

'—especially when that rule is justified by priests and scholars telling us, over and over, that "this is how it has always been". You would have more chance of defending the idea that our river flows uphill than of disobeying Florentine presumptions about marriage.'

'I don't want to marry him!' she said stubbornly.

Leo's blue-eyed gaze held her.

'Then what do you want?' he asked.

Annalisa wondered about that. What *did* she want? To think that she had once been so stupidly besotted with Matteo, a silly, pretentious boy whom she barely knew, whereas . . .

Whereas, now, an impulse! She wanted to swim in the river! Yes, that! To be as naked—wicked thought!—as Leo was in the forest pool, to strike out to the centre where the current was strong and direct, and to be transported by that current. To feel the silken water covering her bare skin like a sleeve, the cold invigorating her, the ancient sky approving her journey! Without the imprisonment of Florence's rules, where would she go? Downstream, of course, floating without stopping beneath bridges and birds, past curious cows and farms and venerable forests to the sea, and then on to new worlds. She would be a disciple of the sunshine, rain, wind, and snow, and a citizen not of Florence but of Everywhere.

A glorious idea, she thought, but one that could not be shared.

Yet.

'I don't know,' she muttered, in answer to his question.

'I think,' said Leo carefully, 'that it is difficult for any of us to know the truth of our desires—'

'You say these things!'

'—because from the time of our birth, when we first open our eyes, we are taught to see our lives through a man-made veil. It is a corruption, like smoke.'

Annalisa felt tears gathering behind her eyes.

'There is smoke,' she agreed. 'Always.'

'Which is why societies do not interest me,' Leo told her. 'Florence does not interest me. I learn from the natural world. Prayer and rule-making have their place, but it is curiosity and observation that will lead us to the truth.'

A fish lifted and plopped as a hawk scythed through the trembling air.

'You blaspheme,' said Annalisa quietly. 'Men have been imprisoned, even killed, for lesser sentiments than that.'

Leo laughed. 'Don't worry,' he said, 'I have my defence prepared.' He cleared his throat, stood tall and spoke in the manner of a pompous lawyer. 'Gentlemen, when we look to the wonders of nature, we are closer than ever to touching the divine. We are closer than ever to God.'

She thought about that while he picked up his notebook and leafed through the pages.

'See here,' he said. 'I've been working on my favourite project.'

Lips sketched into a smile: front-on, side-on, close-up. The detail was remarkable, each version evoking passion, mischief, uncertainty, desire.

The page swam. Annalisa saw her own finger reach out to touch the shapes. She heard Leo's voice running like water through her mind: 'I will make the smile truthful.'

And lovely, she thought as her finger moved slowly over those miraculous lines. Truthful and lovely . . .

And mine.

CHAPTER 14

Lost and Found

Dante threw seed at the chickens, sat behind a giant tussock of weed and remembered.

Three summers ago, lonely as always, he'd wandered away from the village. Glum, without thought, he'd travelled some distance before being distracted by a lark singing from the top of a dung-heap in a meadow. The shrill melody had enchanted him enough that when the bird had left its foul perch and flown to a tree, he had followed it. The lark had teased, flitting back and forth between several trees and singing new tunes, like a siren luring her sailor. When she had flown up and been taken by the light, Dante had farewelled the lark, then looked around and discovered that he was lost.

At first, he hadn't minded. Being lost was better than being at home, listening to his father complain about his various misfortunes and praying that his mother might not succumb to yet another bout of tears. He'd scouted along a series of tracks before realising that shadows were eating into the day and he still had no idea where he was. He'd been walking for over an hour, but the bushes appeared to be the same as before, the valleys sloped the same way, the hills were the same bready, indeterminate shapes and the river remained out of sight.

Panic had tightened his chest, until he'd noticed one difference: a boy sitting with his back against the stone wall of an old shepherd's hut, drawing.

The boy had looked up, saluted elaborately and called for Dante to come over and sit with him. Fighting against his usual shyness, Dante had traipsed up to the hut and squatted nearby. After the standard greetings, he'd shuffled a little closer so he could watch the boy, Leo, draw. Three years hence, and he could still recall that sketch of a galloping horse in great detail. It had been done with such precision that the animal's muscles had seemed to come alive and move as real muscles would move: the lower mouth sagging, the muzzle straining with effort, nostrils flaring and eyes bulging, the mane being rippled by a wind that was undrawn but still somehow there.

'I admire horses,' Leo had told him. 'They have a beautiful structure.'

Dante remembered how unusual it had been for him to hear those words. Most people would've said, without really thinking about it, 'I *love* horses', or possibly, 'I admire horses because they are *noble* or *useful*', but Leo, as he did with all things, had preferred to embrace the physicality, the geometry and the geography of the horse. Not that he was immune to other qualities, having suggested to Dante on a number of occasions since that horses were highly intelligent creatures who doubtless felt many of the same emotions as humans.

'Leo, no!'

'Dante, yes.'

'They are beasts, simple and common. How can they possibly feel—'

'When a horse rides into battle, do you honestly believe that he does so without nerves? Without fear? Of course not! Our horse senses the possibility of injury or worse. His ears prick, his eyes widen, his heart beats faster—'

'I suppose that might happen.'

'A gracious concession, dear friend. Now, consider our warrior's cousin, the humble horse from the paddock. Could it be that he feels boredom at what he must do each day? Or alternately, if he is more generous of spirit, might he feel eagerness, even a sense of worthiness?'

'Who could know?'

'Anyone who is prepared to observe—'

'Observe?'

'—the behaviour of our simple and common beast, to see if there are signs that he feels loyalty to his master, who is kind, or disappointment, because the master is unkind? Signs that this horse might be indifferent or suffering or filled with joy? Dante, ask yourself this. When we observe our horse gazing across the grass, do we presume that he does so because he is a mindless dullard? Or do we consider that he might be dreaming of beautiful things, like a bag of chaff and a cool drink of water, or thinking fondly of the end of his day, or even looking towards another horse and falling in love? I tell you, emotions are not a human invention. Every creature is entitled to feel.'

On that first, remarkable afternoon, Leo had guided Dante back to the Bellomo house. As they had walked, he had begun to open up a new world of possibility, as easily as peeling a piece of fruit.

'Dante, the sky might well be blue, but if you look hard enough, you will see that there are varying shades of blueness and they can change from day to day.

'Examine the bark on that tree and then, tonight, examine the skin on the back of your grandmother's hands. I guarantee you that they will be similar.

'Did you know that when a bee stings you, it cannot do so again? And that soon after, the poor little warrior will die? It is a strange phenomenon. I wonder if the sting might be attached to the bee's gizzards or perhaps even its heart? I must investigate . . .

'See that cloud? That cloud is higher than that cloud. The cloud behind it is higher again. There is no single ceiling of clouds. They are as deeply layered above as rocks are deeply layered below.

'Imagine that there is a river inside your body. This is where your blood is stored. The rivulets that come off the main watercourse are your veins and the streams that come off the rivulets are smaller veins, running close to the skin. You see what this means? The system that moves our blood is the same design as the rivers that move our fish and our ships. Exciting, isn't it?'

From all of this talking and listening came friendship, but Dante was still unable to stop himself from thinking that this wonder had been too easily granted, that it would end when Leo would find other people, cleverer people, and that he, Dante, would return to his lonely life.

Hopefully not for a time. Hopefully not ever!

Time spent with Leo became his saviour. Like all boys of his age, he was expected to better himself through schooling, however learning in the way that society and his father demanded was difficult. Strive as he might, Dante could not grasp the *Aeneid*. Stefano even employed a tutor—'The cost!' he had complained—but despite his great store of knowledge, Signor Pisani, a scholar on sabbatical from Rome, could not instruct, cajole or coerce Dante into knowing more than a few everyday Latin words.

'He reads the letters backwards or upside-down, I cannot tell!' The tutor had become more and more exasperated. After several cups of wine, he and Stefano had agreed to cut short the arrangement. Dante, skulking in the kitchen, had thought, *if Leo was my tutor . . .*

With his schooling thus limited and his father convinced that he was as brainless as a hare, Dante completed his chores as quickly as possible so that he might spend more time with Leo. Still amazed that he had been chosen by this intriguing, smart-mouthed, sharp-eyed boy, he absorbed as much as he could. Being with Leo was not like being in school, because Dante's friend made connections. He unravelled knots. Rather than chastising Dante for reading backwards or upside-down, he found ways of including him in his many endeavours—such as the day Leo had insisted on measuring parts of his body in order to work out the relationships that existed between those parts.

'Dante, lie on the ground and spread your arms as wide as you can.'

'But there are ants!'

'Then we'll have to be quick, before those ants become an army that carries you away like a crust of bread. Come on, I need to check my theory. Yes, like that . . . good. Now, one, two, three . . . one, two, three . . . ah-ha!'

'What?'

'Your arms are as wide as you are tall, Dante. Pretty close, anyway! Now, you must do the same measurements on me. That way, we can begin to prove—'

Here, now, sitting with an itchy back while the chickens clucked and fussed, Dante thought: *if there is no Leo, there is no world for me.*

Scraping sounds, coughing and spitting.

His father said, 'There you are, *pigrone*.'

It was more update than conversation. The villa is sold. We depart in two weeks. You will begin your military training with Gaspare Di Loreto as soon as possible.

A hungry chicken came too close. Stefano used his bad leg to propel the squawking bird into the air.

'Boy,' he growled, 'understand this. I have had to lick one filthy Florentine boot after another to get you this opportunity. You will be a soldier, do you hear me? You are my only son and a Bellomo, and you will be a soldier. That is all.'

That night, as his father snored, Dante's mother came to him, saying, 'Stay quiet and let me tell you . . .'

A story that he had not previously heard about Stefano's own childhood, how *his* father had refused to acknowledge this only son because the boy was lame and therefore of little use in manly pursuits, such as hunting or—

'War?'

'Yes. Dante, your *nonno* was a difficult man. He believed that to have such a child was shameful, that as the head of the Bellomo family he had been unfairly cursed by the Devil. When Stefano was just seven years of age, he was disowned by his father. He grew up in the company of aunts, always hoping to reconcile. Sadly, that never happened, and a few years later his father died, they say from the plague, although that has always been—anyway. Naturally, Stefano was heartbroken, but he hoped that he might at least be able to access some of his father's inheritance and build a new life for himself. However, soon after the funeral, it was discovered that Giovanni had secretly invested his money into silk being transported from Byzantium. The ships had been lost in a storm and the money was gone. Stefano had no choice but to learn his uncle's trade.'

She leaned against her son and went on, 'I was also from a poor family, as you know, so the match was seen as suitable, for who else but a plain and penniless woman would agree to spend their life with an angry saddle-maker who has one leg shorter than the other?'

Dante's insides were taut. He felt the circle of Amara's arms, her tentative kiss on his forehead.

'Some men will always be disappointed with their lives,' she said. 'Your father is one of those men, but he loves you, child. He loves you dearly. It is himself and his past that he dislikes, and neither you nor I will ever change those.'

CHAPTER 15

Impossibilities

The road slithered through ribs and swales. Filthy children skittled and darted, their eyes dark and ghoulish, their hands extended like paws. Fishermen heaved their nets from the Arno. The stench that came from butchers hacking and tanners skinning cut across the breeze. The great walls, with their insets of faded saints and flower-strewn tabernacles, rose high, guards strutted proudly from tower to tower, and finally the mighty gate appeared, ushering Alessandro, Carlotta, Vanni and Annalisa de Torriano back into—

Florence.

Within the city, fanciful young men preened, while curious young women eyed them from the upper windows. Rich families promenaded, the poor trailing behind and scavenging the streets for a dropped coin or morsel of food. Nuns filed in studied silence towards the convent on the hill. Musicians played in a frenzy, hoping for a drink or a meal. The alleyways and squares filled with weavers, wool-makers, goldbeaters and cloth-dyers, with notaries, shopkeepers, merchants and usurers, judges and councillors, physicians and priests, soldiers, shoemakers, poets and preachers.

Flat-eared mules hauled overladen carts. Wild-eyed dogs searched for a fight. Cats harped and scratched. Horses stamped their hooves. Rats raced for their lives. Brawlers, thieves, drunks and almsgivers lurked in the shadows, while in the corners and holes the *mendicanti* squatted like discarded scraps of sackcloth, their limbs drawn in, their eyes downcast.

Sunlit *piazzas* and elegantly spired churches. Tiny shops tucked away like forgotten mementoes, street corners with name-plaques and altars, the mysterious doors and darkly self-important banks, the *bargello*—

Two corpses hung above the street, their bodies swinging in the breeze like stiffened pennants.

'Anna,' said her mother, 'look away, now!'

But it was too late and Annalisa knew that her brief glimpse of those stricken faces would stay in her mind as a permanent imprint of the horror that could, at any time, counteract the city's beauty. Carlotta held her arm and the family sat in silence as the carriage jiggled towards those streets where the mansions were new, their gargoyles clean and their gardens fresh with growth, the final property on the street being the impressively ostentatious House of Piombino.

She thought, *it is natural for them to believe that I am happy.*

They see that their daughter has left the *contado*, where she never wanted to go, and returned to Florence, which she has always loved. They see that she is to be wed to a young man who is, by every account, honourable and ambitious, and that this husband-to-be comes from a family which is well-off and well-connected, all but guaranteeing her future. Moreover, they believe that they have demonstrated the great compass of their love by acting on the single, most important premise of parenting: that of doing what is best for their child.

They see that she is to be steeped in pleasure and pleasantries as well as—their most profound hope—the joys provided by her own children and, one day, grandchildren. They see themselves flushed with the satisfaction that comes from knowing that a job has been done well as, year after year, their daughter resides in a beautiful house in a beautiful city and is surrounded by beautiful objects and people, enjoying a life where she is doted upon and tended as avidly as a prized orchid in the finest of gardens. As Old Age coaxes them into her gentle arms, they see themselves turning to each other proudly and saying: what a superb decision we made! The future of our family is like the future of Florence—golden!

Annalisa thought all of this while she was standing in the Piombino's elaborately decorated *loggia*, with Matteo nearby, as their fathers worked out the details of the alliance. Unable to keep her eyes averted, as she had been instructed, she glanced towards a bronze panel on the wall and recognised guilt-ridden Jephthah turning away from his daughter as she pleaded for his grace. Annalisa closed her eyes and thought, *I am terribly, terribly unhappy.*

As the undisputed heads of their respective families, the two men made little attempt to mask their conversation.

Paolo Piombino drew up his considerable girth and said, 'Since our last meeting, I have confirmed my son's position at Banco dei Medici. He has been in their employment for only a brief time, yet he has already received strong praise from Signor Gatti himself.'

'Very impressive.'

'Yes. We have high hopes. Matteo is a quick learner. Perhaps, one day . . .'

'La Banca di Piombino?'

'Why not, my friend, why not? As Florence grows . . .'

'True enough, and in a city that values progress, there is always room for entrepreneurs. I should tell you, my daughter is also a quick learner. She is most apt.'

'Apt enough to perfect the duties of a major guildsman's wife?'

'Without a doubt. She has learned from the best.'

'I am pleased to hear it. Now, Alessandro, a small matter. Do not be offended, but I am intrigued as to your daughter's complexion. It is somewhat darker than I had realised. If I did not know better, I would guess that she holds, at least in part, the blood of the south?'

'Paolo—'

'I might even have said, *Siciliana*! My little joke, of course.'

'Of course. I appreciate your good humour.'

'I thank you for that compliment. Nevertheless . . .'

'Signor, you must know that I will always be open with you. There is . . . I have to say, there is a southern—a remote lineage on her mother's side.'

'Really? And yet, Alessandro, this was not mentioned at our previous meetings? Nor did her portrait indicate such a—how do I phrase this?—such a feature.'

'Paolo—'

'It goes without saying that we expect our paintings to be truthful depictions. Was the artist, perhaps, incompetent?'

'No, no, he is a fine practitioner: I would not employ anyone who is not of the highest standard. This was—an oversight. My daughter's link with the south is distant enough to be inconsequential, hence my decision not to acknowledge or portray it. That said, I can only apologise. It was a thoughtless omission.'

'I thank you for your candour.'

'Under the circumstances, candour is the least I can offer. Paolo, I hope that—'

'Alessandro, do not fret! It is of no great concern. There is beauty enough; in fact your daughter is exquisite to the eye, to every eye, I should think. My son is a lucky man! Am I right in supposing that the Neapolitan temper has been bred out of her?'

'Most assuredly.'

'Excellent. Obedience is paramount. Forgive me, but I have one more question. Your own lovely wife, she was a young mother?'

Alessandro nodded. 'Yes,' he said, 'although a younger bride—'

'Of course.'

'—if only by nine months!'

Both men laughed.

As they joined hands and cemented the deal, Paolo Piombino said, 'A history of fertility is encouraging. You understand how it is. We are anxious for grandchildren and Matteo, our eldest son, is equally anxious to provide for our wishes.'

'Of course,' said Alessandro de Torriano. 'I fully understand how it is.'

The families joined for a celebratory feast. The highlight of the meal was the serving of huge segments of a roasted stag that Annalisa could not eat.

'Is the girl unwell?'

'Anna?'

'Father, I am sorry. The excitement of returning to the city has upset my stomach.'

'Take some wine, girl. That will ease your indigestion.'

They spoke of the sumptuous bridal chest, the parade, the church.

'August, then?'

'As discussed, yes.'

Finally, they allotted Matteo and Annalisa time to speak with each other through a window, as custom allowed, with their mothers sitting nearby as chaperones.

He passed her a small, gold pendant with a peridot inset and said, very formally, 'I look forward to our wedding day.'

Annalisa accepted the pendant and handed over the silk scarf that her father had provided. She tried in vain to catch his eyes.

'You are a banker?' she hissed. 'What happened to the Academy? What about learning Greek and writing poetry?'

'Idle pursuits,' he muttered, still avoiding her gaze.

'Noble, wonderful pursuits,' she said fiercely, but Matteo did not respond.

They stood on either side of the casement, silent and pinch-faced, until the doors burst open and their merry fathers ended the meeting.

Normally Annalisa would have looked forward to the feast day of Saint John, especially the horse race where, amid much excitement, the beasts galloped the perimeter of the city. Today, however, a lack of sleep had left her tired and irritable, meaning that she could not hold her tongue when her father insisted that, with Luca looking after the estate, the family could certainly remain in Florence for the festivities, perhaps longer.

'Father, can we please return to the *contado*?'

Alessandro snorted.

'Wife,' he said to Carlotta, 'is this our Anna? She who could not *bear* to leave Florence—'

'Please?' she implored.

'No,' said Alessandro. He wiped his lips. 'We will stay here.'

'Father, I beg you!'

'Your begging is unnecessary. We will remain in Florence.'

'Please? Even for a short time—'

'Anna, I have already said no! Why do you counter me on this?'

Vanni came to her.

'Sister,' he said quietly, 'favour me with a walk.'

'Go,' Carlotta told him briskly. 'Talk some manners into her.'

They headed for quieter streets. Annalisa sensed rain, the Florentine type, bloody and smoke-stained. Her tiredness made her joints ache, but worse was the flurry in her mind, last night's dreams reappearing.

Dead animals falling from the sky. A pale child plunging into black water and re-emerging as a skeleton. Pairs of bloodless lips grinning like death-masks as they left the *bargello* and flew towards her face.

She trooped along behind Vanni. Briefly, stupidly, she wondered if she was going mad.

Inside the nave of the great *basilica*, she approached the altar and prayed with genuine intent. When they left the church, the rain had arrived, forcing them to shelter within one of the arcades.

Vanni said, 'Do you really miss the *contado*?'

Annalisa nodded. Despite her pleas to God, she felt miserable. Why did her life have to turn in this direction? Trapped into a marriage she didn't want, her future as dull and predictable as any boring tapestry . . .

'And the boy,' said Vanni. 'You miss him too?'

Annalisa stared at her brother.

'What boy? You mean, my chaperone?'

'No,' he said softly, 'the other. The singer, the artist. Anna, I have seen you with him. I doubt that you noticed me; your engagement was elsewhere.'

She could feel her face tingling, but there was concern in Vanni's eyes.

'You love him?'

'I don't know,' she admitted. 'He . . . enchants me.'

'Love or enchantment,' said Vanni, 'either way, it is impossible.'

Irritated, she moved away.

'What would you know?'

'I know enough.'

'You know about money and gaming and father's business, but I doubt that you know of love.'

'So, you admit it? This is love?'

She was silent, fuming. Vanni sighed.

He said, 'Anna, as your eldest brother, let me offer you some advice.'

'I don't need—'

'A life guided by reason is far more pleasurable and easier to navigate than one which succumbs to emotion.'

'You really believe that?'

'Of course.'

'Then use your own reason and leave! I will find my own way home.'

'You know I cannot do that. Sister, think for a moment. Think about what we have! Our house and villa, our friends, father's wealth and, most importantly, our family. Our successful family! Why do we have these things? Because we are prepared to follow the Florentine way.'

'Dear Vanni,' she said bitterly, 'always a stickler for the rules.'

'And why not? You cannot rightly enjoy the benefits of

success if you are not prepared to contribute.'

'By marrying outside of love?'

'By marrying strategically and building the strength of the Torriano legacy.'

'Oh, you are your father's son, Vanni!'

'No, I am loyal to family and city, and I understand what is required to maintain the status of both.'

'You understand nothing! You know nothing!'

'Anna, listen to me—'

'I refuse!'

'There is no choice,' Vanni told her as the rain intensified. 'Unless you wish to become an outcast, you must marry Matteo Piombino. Believe me: Florence does not offer any better alternative for you, and Italy does not offer any better alternative than Florence.'

CHAPTER 16

Truth and Illusion

When Dante was a small child, his mother had taken him to the village of Minervo, where she'd been born and spent most of her childhood. On the way, she'd told him that the lady they were visiting was called Bettina.

Amara had said, 'She was my nurse, but I came to think of her as my mother.'

Her real mother had died giving premature birth to Amara's brother. A day later, unable to draw breath into lungs as narrow as fish gills, the boy had also died. Three-year-old Amara and her grieving father had stayed alone in the cottage, until a determined rapping had led Amara to climb onto a stool and unlatch the door.

Bettina's appearance was hard and leathery. She was knotted like the trunk of an ancient oak, but she smelled of chamomile and had the playful, inquisitive gaze of a goat skipping across hills. As Bettina had entered the cottage, carrying a linen sack with a cherry-coloured rope, little Amara had wondered if the woman was a spirit who had come from another village, or the forest, or even a different world.

'Dear child,' Bettina had said. The kindness in her voice had surprised Amara. 'Come here so that I can wash your face clean and make it ready for tomorrow, and all the tomorrows after that.'

Amara's father had raised himself from his miserable stoop and croaked, 'Who sent you?'

Bettina had replied, 'The village, of course, who else?'

Years later, Amara had explained to Dante, 'Minervo is a tiny village and the same families have lived there, year in, year out, since Jesus was in His cradle. Everybody knows and understands each other. If people fight, the village insists that they stop. If a parent dies, the village finds someone to look after the children. That is how it has always been, and how it should always be.'

To get to Minervo, they'd crossed streams and meadows dotted with nettles and yarrow, and passed through fields of sunflowers that shook beneath a multitude of beating wings. Once there, they'd been directed to a small abbey nestled between groves of olive trees. A nun had taken them to Bettina. The old lady was ill, her body like an ash-heap on her cot.

She'd opened her one good eye, gazed at Dante and told Amara, 'He's as pretty as you were.' An hour later, she was with her Maker.

The nuns had allowed Amara and Dante to stable their

horse and cart, and to sleep in the pressing-room behind the abbey. The next day, at Bettina's funeral, the cloistered air inside the chapel and the long, complicated service had made it difficult for Dante to maintain his attention. His gaze had wandered to the frescoes and this was when he had first seen an image of the angel Raphael with Tobias, son of Tobit of Nineveh, and been captivated by them and later by their story.

Now, as he sat on the crest of a hill, he looked at the only world that he had properly known and thought, *I will be like Tobias who journeys afar and returns, many years hence, to cure his father of blindness. My own father's blindness being me and my future . . . Before that, however, I will honour my mother's village by walking the length and breadth of Italy so that I can tell people to stop fighting and to look after each other's children.*

He closed his eyes and prayed that God would forgive him for abandoning his mother and defying his father's wishes, and he prayed that the angel Raphael would be sent to protect him, as God had allowed with Tobias. As he prayed, time dripped like rain onto the pebbles and the grass, until Dante heard footsteps and Leo's voice flowing like a warm wind.

'Dante, I found you! You're here. You're here!'

Was this the right time, he wondered? Over and over, he

had rehearsed the conversation.

'Leo, I must leave.'

'Dear friend, go home if you wish. I will see you tomorrow.'

'No, I mean leave *here*. Vinci, the *contado*. I must go to Florence.'

'But you will return?'

'No. I am to join the military. My father insists.'

This was the point at which Dante became less certain. How would Leo respond? Would he say indignantly, 'Well, I insist otherwise!' or 'We'll soon change that!' or even, greatest hope of all, 'My Uncle Francesco has offered you a place in our house and your father has agreed.' Or would he surprise by suggesting, 'This much is certain; you must obey your parents,' or using that booming voice to proclaim, 'O Great Bellomo, you will be a brave and wonderful soldier!' Or, horror of horrors, might Leo offer words such as these, 'Farewell, I have enjoyed our friendship, but now it is done,' before turning away, notebook in hand, eyes firmly focused on the dazzling light of his own future?

Oh, the fear of being forced into knowing the unknown: it slid into his heart like steel! No prayer could prevent that.

Dante decided to keep the conversation for later. For now, it was better to sit with his friend and allow the palette of the countryside to soak into him like dye. Leo was unusually subdued and the breeze that seesawed across this part of the Earth was laden with music, as if God's dulcimer played beneath the grass and behind the clouds.

Dante closed down. He felt white and empty. Everything inside him, every drop of blood, chunk of flesh and troublesome thought seeped into the thirsty soil so that, for a time at least, he considered nothing, imagined nothing, became nothing.

Until Leo said unexpectedly, 'Friend, I need your eyes.'

Dante shook himself awake. Leo was sitting upright, as alert as any sentinel as he gazed west.

'My eyes?'

'Yes, for an experiment. I want you to look to the precise point where I am looking.'

'To the hills?'

'Further. As far as you can see. Let me guide you. Do you spy that field of rapeseed?'

'Yes.'

'And above? A group of buildings?'

'I see something like buildings.'

'And over the buildings, do you see the spire of a church?'

'Ah . . . yes, I think so.'

'Good. Tell me, how does that spire look to you?'

'It is barely visible, but . . . like any spire, I suppose. Tall, thin—'

'But is it clear? Do you see details? Pieces of shale, perhaps, or a slight bow in the angle of the stones?'

'I see a spire,' Dante told him. 'That is all.'

'So, the details do not exist? This is a spire without shale or bowed angles?'

'Leo, I cannot know—'

'You cannot know because, like me, you cannot see that closely. No matter that our vision is as young and excellent as we are, the spire is too far away. What we see is much smaller and less detailed than what is really there. Agreed?'

Dante nodded. Leo was obviously excited by his observation.

He said, 'So, the distance distorts our view, but, Dante, here is the thing. It is not just the distance.'

'No?'

'No, it is the air!'

'The air?'

'Yes! We think of air as clear or invisible, but it is not. There are things *inside* air, tiny pieces of the world which interrupt our vision.'

'What things?'

'Oh, there are many. Specks of grit. Fragments of stone and shell, pollen drifting from petals and leaves, the dust raised by animals, steam and mist lifting from the oceans and rivers, vapours that pour forth, unnoticed, from the bowels of the Earth . . . no matter how much we might believe otherwise, we can never see an object exactly as it is because, between our eyes and that object, there must always be air!'

'With things inside?'

'Yes! Dante, do you see what this means?'

'Um . . .'

'It means that just as things exist in truth because they are there, in front of us, so do they also exist as illusions. There is the object itself, in its own unique form, and then there is the object that we perceive! These are related, obviously, but one does not simply imitate the other. No, no, no! They are minutely different, because to the human eye, everything is seen through an ever-changing filter . . . of what, Dante?'

'Air?'

'Yes! Yes, yes, yes!'

He was on his feet now, stamping about like an impatient horse.

'It is the same with colours,' he exclaimed. 'It must be! To our eyes, the colour of something—Dante, quickly! Nominate an object!'

'Um, a flower.'

'Good! What type of flower?'

'A—a rose.'

'Perfect! A rose is the paragon of flowers! Now, picture this. Our rose is clearly red, yet that lovely colour appears to fade as we move away from her, a piece of trickery that is caused by the intervention of—you guessed it!—air. She is still red, but we must look through unclear air and thus our rose appears in a different shade!' Leo opened his arms wide as if to embrace the chest of the world, then he cried, 'The sky overhead is blue. But look, the sky that lines the horizon is nearly white—and yet they are the same sky! The air does all of this and so we are immersed—immersed, Dante!'

'Immersed?'

'Yes! In illusion!'

He was so excited that Dante could do no more than follow him, running in celebration down the hill and through the pastures until they reached the river, where Leo had left his notebook beneath a stone. Dante watched as his friend scribbled frantically, then danced along the banks, singing notes that were too strange to attract words, until, finally, when they reached the stone-wall markings of Vinci, Leo announced again, 'It is the air, the air!' before turning and saying, quite matter-of-factly, 'By the way, did I tell you? We are soon to do another performance and it will be our best yet!'

He hugged Dante and skipped triumphantly away. Dante watched him go. *Yes*, he thought, *we will do another performance and your brilliance will shine like the sun. I will be with you one last time and then I will be gone, not to Florence as my father wants, but slipping through your precious air to somewhere not yet known. I will be alone in the morass of the world and praying for the help of a tender-winged angel.*

He saw that Leo was about to enter the village and thought: *dear friend, will you care that I am gone? Or are we an illusion too?*

CHAPTER 17

Resolutions

Her mother said to her, 'Anna, it's a lovely day. Shall we go to the garden and take some air?'

Annalisa sniffed her disdain—no day could be lovely and no air worth taking when she was being forced to marry that dull dreg—but she followed her mother to the garden, recently upgraded at considerable expense. From the archway entrance, she could see trails of ivy criss-crossing the stone walls that surrounded the geraniums and hedges. Laurel trees guarded irises and primroses, while a gravel path slid through the garden's spine towards a courtyard with a fountain featuring Alessandro's favourite statue, Apollo, readying himself to play the *kithara*. Tucked behind the fountain was a row of lemon trees flanked by beds that overflowed with fennel, peppermint, elderflowers and caraway.

Not so long ago, Annalisa would have been entranced by such a space. Now the garden's aromas verged on poisonous and the garish colours romped like clowns. How could this artificial quadrangle compete with the forest near Vinci, with its lovely, green-shadowed cataract and ancient cave? How could a city garden—no matter how carefully planned—hope to compare favourably with the grandeur of a river and those sweeping hills and sweet-smelling meadows?

Simple answer: it couldn't.

She sat with her mother on a bench and watched the water rushing towards Apollo's feet, as if the god of healing sought to revitalise his song within the ripples. As birds twittered and sunlight filtered through the laurel leaves, Florence receded.

Carlotta said, 'Daughter, listen to me. I felt the same way.'

Annalisa looked up and saw that her mother's mouth was tight, as if she was reliving some kind of pain.

'I was frightened,' Carlotta continued. 'Before my marriage.' She leaned in and lowered her voice. 'Utterly terrified.'

Annalisa couldn't imagine her strong and decisive mother ever being like that.

She thought for a moment before saying, 'But you told Father that you were happy. Mother, I heard you. *Bliss*. That was the word. You were blissful.'

As if God had consecrated their union before it had even happened.

'Men are at peace when their beliefs are restated by

others,' said Carlotta smoothly. 'Husbands in particular.'

So, her mother was *not* blissful?

'I was frightened,' said Carlotta again, 'as you now are, because so much was unknown. *All*, perhaps, was unknown. The mind hosts many questions. Will I be a suitable bride? Will I learn how to be a wife? Will he ever regret this choice? I kept thinking: I know so little. How will I cope if I know so little? But, for all the questioning, I still understood that it was my God-given duty and great fortune to marry your father.' Carlotta laced her long fingers. 'I accepted my duty and embraced my fortune. I continue to do so.'

Annalisa knew that she was being intrusive, but she had to ask.

'Do you love him?'

'Oh, yes! Silly child, of course I do.'

Relief. Her parents were no lie.

'If love develops from an expanding knowledge of the other,' Carlotta added, 'which I think it does. If it develops from that, and tolerance and respect, but most of all from the feeling that this person is as much a part of you as any other part and you cannot contemplate the loss of them—if love is the sum of all of these qualities, then yes. You see, Anna, I do love your father, deeply as it happens.' She smiled in that fleeting way that she had and said, 'But when the betrothal was announced and we met for the first time, I was afraid. As you are.'

Annalisa lowered her eyes. It was ridiculous, but

she felt momentarily sad for this earlier version of her mother. Nothing scared Carlotta de Torriano! She was the touchstone, the one who balanced—at times with the ferocity of a cornered cat—the swaying humours of her husband and children. That she would ever know *fear* . . .

A light breeze slipped through, shivering the purple from the irises.

Carlotta asked, 'Shall I tell you how I overcame my concerns?'

Despite herself, Annalisa nodded.

Her mother said, 'Dearest heart, through understanding. Through coming to appreciate the truth about love: that it is no instantaneous flash, as the poets insist, but learned. Mark that word. Love is *learned.* Do you see what I mean?'

Another nod, to confirm her understanding. Her mother seemed satisfied.

She said, 'If there is someone else, perhaps, for whom you feel a more *instant* affection, be certain that this is neither unusual for a girl of your age, nor of any consequence. The feeling will pass. When it does, and you have learned of the steady and reliable nature of proper love, that will be as fulfilling as anything else that you experience in what will hopefully be a long and much blessed life.'

Steady. *Reliable*. The words seemed immovable, like boulders.

'Anna, your father is correct,' Carlotta told her. 'You will grow to love Matteo as he will grow to love you. The two of you will be like plants taken from separate gardens and seeded into a single plot. Over time, your branches will entwine, your fears will subside and you will reflect upon them as childish and capricious—a reflection that, in the future, you may well share with your own daughter. For now, though, re-open your eyes to the light of our family and the corresponding light of Florence. In your current state, you may see happiness as elusive, but I can assure you that reconsidering your situation and being grateful for what your father has done for you will lead to a much healthier state of mind.'

Following her mother's counsel, Annalisa decided to at least appear to re-attune herself to life behind the high walls. She was quiet and compliant in fulfilling her obligations. She read, sewed and prayed, and she practised her dance-steps and the lyre. When the Piombinos visited, she responded to Matteo's clumsy attempts at chivalry with measured doses of modesty and admiration. After they had departed, she overheard her father say to his wife, 'Your advice was well-received.'

'Husband,' said Carlotta, 'Annalisa is a good daughter. Do not doubt her.'

'She is a good daughter because she has a good

mother. That much is obvious.'

'I commend your kindness. Is the contract signed?'

'Yes, and returned to the notary. I have engaged Ser Piero. He is well-recommended.'

At night, when she was supposed to be asleep, Annalisa lay prone beneath the summer heat and tried to imagine marriage to a successful young banker. Would they always live with his family or one day have a villa of their own? If so, what about servants? Presumably there would be some, but how many and who would select them? Would she be expected to entertain? How did one organise such matters? And what of children? How many and at what intervals?

These were troubling questions, made more so because whenever she tried to picture herself as a wife and mother, other images intervened: a golden-haired boy singing to the stars, her strange but welcome coronation as Queen of the Forest, the glorious sight of six freed birds soaring over the village . . . The sketch beneath her bed; what she saw as the beatification of her smile. Leo's bright, restless eyes unravelling the world, following her into the next day, and the one after that.

Then, a surprise. The family was seated for dinner when her father announced a return to their villa for the local festival to mark the summer grain harvest.

'*Brief* return.' He looked across the table at Annalisa and smirked. 'We cannot stay too long. I hear that there is a wedding in August, a very important wedding.'

'I can go, if you wish,' Vanni offered. 'I am happy to help Luca with the organisation of the harvest.'

'No, we will all go.' Alessandro leaned forward and ripped a wing from a roasted pigeon. 'As a landowner, it is important that I be seen at the festival.'

'Father, I would welcome the opportunity.'

'No doubt you would. But I have decided otherwise and we will all go. Be assured, Vanni, your brother is doing as well as can be expected.'

'You have heard from Luca?' Vanni's words carried an underlay of peevishness. He added, 'I have not had a single word.'

'And why should you?' said Alessandro with sudden, unannounced aggression. 'You are his brother; I am his father! Where might reports go?'

'Father, I did not mean to undermine you.'

'Oh, you did not? Then be silent, if you cannot be sensible or respectful!' Alessandro's brusque order was meant for them all. He tossed away the wing-bone and muttered, 'Anyway, my sources keep me well enough informed.'

Annalisa eyed her father as he continued to consume vast quantities of food. Her mother chewed with her usual precision, but Vanni, obviously unsettled by the exchange, picked at the offerings on his plate. She could guess why. She, too, felt uneasy. *My sources keep me well enough informed . . . You're spying on him*, she thought. *You're spying on your own son!* Luca, as good-humoured and fresh-faced as a puppy, was being secretly monitored by his father.

Why? There could only be one reason.

Because he was not trusted.

She saw it now. This second-rate village festival was an excuse. No-one would care whether or not Alessandro de Torriano was there. No, the family was returning to Vinci to check on Luca, to make sure that he really was doing 'as well as can be expected'. Her brother hadn't been left to run their small estate as an obligation or favour; it was a test. As if to say: there are doubts that need to be dispelled, so we will try this as a way of gathering evidence about the true character of the boy.

His flesh and blood. His son!

And what of their mother? Annalisa glanced across the table at the dark-haired, dark-eyed woman who sat stiff-backed, eyes down, lips barely separated as they took in tiny morsels of food. *You know*, she thought. *You know and you approve!*

Was this, then, the truth of what marriage becomes? Love—if it even exists—dissolves into a political partnership? Two plants twist into one then turn against the world, even their own family.

This very Florentine form of treachery!

Her father belched loudly, thrust away his plate

and left the table. Shortly after, Vanni stood and went through the outer door. Carlotta signalled and Martina began to clear the plates.

'Daughter,' said Carlotta, 'will you work on your sewing?'

She murmured her assent. But Annalisa was not considering stitches. *Luca*, she thought, *is my closest, my favourite. He must be told. And when he knows of the actions of our parents, he will surely be resolved, like me, to act.*

Two against the world. Luca will not be doubted. I will not marry Matteo Piombino.

CHAPTER 18

'Dante,' he had said, 'if I am to become the artist that I wish to become—'

'That is, "the best of all time".'

'Your memory is faultless. If I am to reach my destiny, then I must better understand the primary subject matter of all great art.'

'Which is?'

'Humans, of course!'

'What more do you need to know of humans?'

'Everything! Our hopes and our loves, our fears, how our minds work, how our bodies are made—'

'Our bodies?'

'Dante, you seem amazed when I am simply stating the obvious. If I am to improve my art, then I must have a greater knowledge of the human body—'

'I suppose so.'

'—beginning with our bones.'

'Our bones?'

'Excellent! Your hearing is as good as your memory.'

'But Leo, our bones sit beneath our flesh. They are not—'

'Available? Not easily, no. However, the fact remains that knowing about bones is vital to the craft of the artist. Understanding their shapes and sizes will help me to see how the tendons and sinews are placed *around* them, and how the muscles interact *with* them. Help me to see patterns of movement! Just as a builder needs to know about timber and stone, and a banker needs to know about numbers, an artist needs to know about bones. Agreed?'

'Ye-es.'

'Good. Then you will also agree that we need to locate some.'

'Bones?'

'Correct again.'

'Do you mean . . . from the dead?'

'Of course, from the dead! Dante, why so obtuse? Surely you can see that my quest is best served by examining the bones of those who have died rather than those who remain alive. I can hardly ask you or anyone else to slice open your flesh and deliver me a rib or a radius, can I? This is why we will visit the ossuary.'

'Where the dead lie?'

'The long-dead, yes. Dear friend, I can see already that this little excursion worries you, but think of it this way. Bones are merely objects. They are as harmless as sticks.'

'But the souls—'

'Have long departed. You might just as well walk into an empty house.'

A convenient argument, he'd thought, *but what of Florence's laws? What of God's laws?*

That conversation had occurred this morning. Now it was very late and Dante was in his room, trembling as he awaited Leo's signal, because entering an ossuary after midnight to look at bones was definitely a sin, no matter how artistically arguable the motivation might be.

I will be caught, he thought gloomily. *I will be convicted as a criminal and I will be either hanged or burned. My mother will weep unchecked for the rest of her life and my father . . . Who knows what my father will do?*

There was a scraping noise, the rattle of a pebble striking the wall, followed by a low whistle. He looked outside. In the demi-light, Leo's face was astral and compelling.

'Come on!' he whispered.

Did I even agree to this? thought Dante. *Or, once again, does he presume?*

'Dante! Hurry!'

Grimacing at his own weakness, he whispered an apology to the Almighty, lifted himself onto the sill and eased out of the window. An excited Leo helped him down. They waited a moment to check that Dante's departure was undetected, then Leo led him into a night made of sylvan shadows and unfamiliar sounds.

The ossuary, behind the church, was a small but dignified structure. Leo insisted that it would be easily entered because, apart from priests and those who transported the remains of the departed, no-one wanted to go inside such a building.

'I checked yesterday,' he said. 'The door is held by a crossbeam. It is heavy, but not immoveable.'

The air was crisp, the moonlight radiant. Tiny candles of blue and gold fell from the heavens and stippled the trees, spilling any leftover light onto the tombstones in the graveyard. The boys crept past the church nave, Dante consciously avoiding any accusatory stares from the saints. They were close to the sacristy when—

'Aroowww!'

His heart leapt as he cried out and stumbled into Leo's back.

'What was that?'

'Just a cat.' Leo helped Dante regain his balance. 'Fear not, O Great Bellomo,' he whispered. 'We will survive the cat, just as we will survive any other demons or basilisks that Satan may choose to send.'

They walked on, Dante feeling sick to his core. The ossuary loomed. Leo went to the doors and heaved the crossbeam. The grinding sound seemed to bounce hard into the heavens.

'Leo, it's too loud!'

'Relax, my friend, relax! Everyone is asleep. If they hear anything, they'll think of it as a dream.'

With one side of the door freed, there was space enough for them to squeeze through.

'A torch,' said Dante desperately. 'We need a torch! Leo, without that—'

'If anyone does happen to stir, then a torch will reveal our whereabouts.' Leo pointed towards the sky. 'Look, the moon favours us and there is at least one high window to allow its light.'

'But—'

'Be strong!' Leo grabbed Dante's arm and hauled him into the ossuary. The air was colder than outside and smelled like sour milk. Leo began to descend the stone steps, but Dante pulled back and stayed close to the half-opened door. As his eyes adjusted to the gloom, he saw shelves hammered onto the walls, each one providing a final home to several skeletons. The skulls, ribs and limbs were mostly connected, but some had been pulled apart and scattered.

'Rats,' said Leo, 'those intemperate disturbers of the peace.' He sounded more bemused than annoyed.

Still feeling sick, Dante watched as his friend edged towards one of the shelves, surveyed briefly, extracted a long, pale bone and held it up like a trophy of war.

'Behold, the ulna!'

He began to inspect the bone, turning it over and over, and running his finger along its smooth shape. Despite his own trepidation, Dante could not prevent himself from watching.

Such a strangeness, he thought, *to know that this brittle-looking thing had once given strength to an arm!* He wondered, before reaching its final resting place, what had that arm done? Had it dug and planted? Jiggled reins and herded animals? Wielded the axe and sword, perhaps, or raised the rigging of a ship? Lifted food to hungry mouths, fingers to lips, children to the sun? Gripped a lifetime of friends or rested quietly, with only its owner for company?

And what of the end? Had this arm rebelled against its demise by waving away time and beating hard against a bed of straw, or lain itself open to God as if to say, Lord, I have done my duty and now it is time for me to go?

'Yes,' said Leo, 'that seems about right.' He was comparing the lengths of several bones.

Dante swallowed hard. 'I think we should leave,' he said.

'Not yet.'

'Leo—'

'Why leave when we've only just arrived? Dante, look. This is fascinating! The length of this femur suggests that its owner was remarkably tall, whereas—'

'But we're trespassing!' An unaccustomed passion had

grown within him. 'Leo, these are not mere objects, as you describe them. They are people. They have—*had* lives. It doesn't seem right to be here, examining their bones like . . .'

Like we were in a marketplace, he thought. *A grisly, sinful marketplace.*

'Dante,' said Leo in a priestly tone, 'the artist works for God by depicting His wonders. Given that humans can reasonably be classified as being among those wonders, surely God will accept that a little research is needed if I am to be accurate in my depictions?'

'I'm not talking about God,' said Dante fiercely. He wanted to add, how can you possibly know what God does or doesn't accept? Who has the right to know that?

Finally, Leo looked up.

'What, then?'

'People,' Dante told him. 'Respect.'

He thought of his *nonna*, Ludovica; how difficult she had been, how much he had loved her. Ludovica, who lay in the nearby graveyard, melting and separating.

Leo pushed the bones carefully back onto their shelves and came closer.

'You see this as disrespectful?'

Yes, he thought, *because there has to be some . . . distance.* Wasn't that Leo's own idea? If the illusion can never properly match that which is real, surely it followed that the work of the artist, also an illusion, could never—and should never—match the life and truth of the subject?

As if the bones and their owners might rightfully say: interpret us if you wish, but do not have the arrogance to think that you can recreate us, wholly and absolutely.

Oh Leo, he thought. *You need to remember that there is only one Creator.*

One.

'Dante, tell me.'

He deliberated before saying, 'I think it is better, and kinder, to learn from the living than to interrupt the dead.'

He expected argument, but Leo rested his palm on Dante's arm and he saw that there was something different in his friend's face, a new form of recognition.

'You may well be right,' said Leo. 'In which case, we must go.'

They sat together in a field. The cold grass made their legs tingle, while the moon on their faces was a fresh and beautiful light. The wild deer that grazed nearby murmured and rustled like old souls. Away from the ossuary, in this more pristine world, Dante finally felt safe enough to tell Leo about his father's edict: Florence, military school, life as a soldier, the planned restoration of the Bellomo name.

Leo listened, then he said, 'You are not that person.'

Encouraged, Dante told him more: his alternate plan

to be like Tobias, son of Tobit of Nineveh, who had set out bravely on his own journey.

But Leo said, 'You are not that person, either.'

Frustration, like a dart.

'Nor am I the Great Bellomo,' Dante chided him, 'yet you insist on naming me in that way.'

Thus separated, they turned from each other and looked out. There was a relenting in the sky: dawn poised on the horizon, awaiting her turn.

'You have given me fair advice tonight,' Leo said. 'Allow me to do the same for you. Dante, you are a gentle person. Let that gentleness be your guide.'

At the edges of the world, it seemed that someone had lit a low fire, the darkness turning to rose then orange, a thin line of ivory emerging like a cautious spirit.

'The new sky binds us to the old Earth.' Leo's voice could've been anywhere.

As the sky's colours animated and the birds sent out their first, grateful notes, the light of grace came before the sun, like a child stirring ahead of its parent. That light nudging the pearly hem of the field was a signal for both boys to stand, blink away the darkness and creep soundlessly home.

CHAPTER 19

Directions

Inside the jolting carriage, her father had amused himself by teasing Annalisa about their return to the 'dreaded' *contado*. Her mother's face had remained a mask. Vanni had spent the entire journey with his eyes down or focused on the outer world. It was a relief, then, to arrive at their villa, rush to the *loggia* and absorb, once again, the welcome sight of the meadows, the river and that lovely and beguiling forest.

Where was he? she wondered, *Observing? Exploring? Experimenting? Sketching? No matter, he would certainly be at the summer festival and perhaps . . .*

Perhaps.

Late afternoon, using the lure of an untold secret, she was able to manoeuvre Luca down to the old well. The sun had been at its whitest and most molten throughout the day, and her brother, who'd spent hours riding the fields and supervising preparations for the harvest, gleamed with the sweat and pleasure of exertion.

'A secret?' he said. 'Quickly, then, out with it.'

Annalisa shook her head. 'Walk with me,' she murmured. The villa was too close, the air too still.

'How mysterious you are.' Rather than walk, Luca was leaning against the well, with a broad grin on his face.

'Anna,' he said, 'what do you see in this well?'

Another game, she thought. *Play along—for now.*

'I see what is before us.'

'Which is?'

'Are you blind? Poor fellow, I must help you. There is a spindle, a rope, a bucket and—look, there is even water.'

'And that is all?'

'That is all.'

'No, dear heart, you are wrong! There is more, much more, for this is no ordinary well!'

He laughed and told her that fairies lived in a city below the well—'A great city, greater even than Florence!' He said that if, at a precise and twilit instant, you were to look upon the water, rather than see your own reflection, the entrancing gaze of the fairies would greet you and draw you down against your will. You would not drown, but you would be taken into the city and there you would stay until it was your turn to go back to the well, look up with your new fairy eyes and draw down another.

'What a strange—and untrue—story you tell.'

'The sun will soon be low. Prove me wrong, if you wish.'

'Luca,' she said, 'enough. Please, listen to me.'

She edged away from the villa. This time, Luca did go with her, and she told him quickly: our father spies upon you. He has people who watch you and send him information. There can only be one conclusion, that you are not trusted.

'It is wrong,' she insisted, 'terribly wrong! You are his son!'

Luca disengaged her arm and went to the stone wall that separated the Torriano fields from those of their neighbour. Annalisa followed. Down here, closer to wildflowers and the untamed grass, she could smell the old, hardscrabble bitterness of the soil.

'Second son,' said Luca firmly.

'What does that matter? You are family. You should be trusted!'

'Sweet Anna.' He folded his arms. 'How naïve you are. This is about birth, not trust.'

His version was spoken with a meld of bitterness and resignation that alarmed her. The second son can never hope to equal the first son, nor, for that matter, the first and in this case only daughter. Vanni, he said, must tread in the footsteps of our father. For him, a great responsibility: the family's fortune.

You, Annalisa, are the jewel that glows ardently in the eyes of both parents. For you, also, a great responsibility: the family's continuance. For both of you, an underscore: the family's honour.

'Which brings us to the second son,' he said. 'This star-crossed creature spends the early part of his life hoping for a role where he too may offer his family the benefit of honour. However, given the standard assumption—mostly by fathers—that a second son is more likely to rebel against his unfortunate placement and offer *dishonour*, this becomes a forlorn hope. Hence, two choices: to fulfil that assumption of dishonour, or to deny it. Opting for the latter, the second son may become a soldier. He may be scholarly or he may learn a trade. Or he may be removed from Florence's distractions and told to administer some far-flung section of the family estate. If he does this and, in the manner of a dog, stays loyal and compliant—and turns a profit—then this second son may come to be regarded as an asset. Assets, of course, are not necessarily honourable, but they are useful in that they have an economic value. So, you see, Anna, for the second son, economic usefulness is the pinnacle of achievement.'

He sat on the wall and turned his face to the sun's embers, and she was reminded of a time in their childhoods, she being no more than six years of age, Luca beginning to stretch into his limbs, Vanni bristling towards early manhood. Uncle Bernardo had presented the boys with wooden swords. Immediately, they had wanted to demonstrate their prowess. Annalisa recalled Vanni as being especially keen. The men had laughed and encouraged them, but everyone had been surprised when the ensuing duel had favoured Luca, the younger boy being quicker on his feet and more accurate with his attack.

It could've ended there. But the next morning, Annalisa had seen, through a window, Alessandro teaching Vanni better swordplay. Father and son had practised vigorously while the other, second son sat against a wall and watched. He may have been disconsolate or perhaps accepting; she hadn't known. But that afternoon, when Vanni had cockily offered him another duel, Luca had refused and walked away.

Annalisa remembered the response, Vanni yelling, 'You're a coward!' and brandishing his wooden sword like a Roman tribune. Yet it had been the hollowest of victories.

'Luca,' she said, 'listen to me. You are no dog, nor are you merely an *asset*. You are their son! First, second, fifth, tenth; the number makes no difference.'

'Oh, but it does.' He came back to her then and she was shocked to see dampness beneath the eyes of her normally cheerful, mischievous brother. She touched his arm, and he offered her a weak smile and said, 'Anna, I will tell you this, but you must say nothing to our parents, to Vanni, no-one.'

He was leaving. As soon as it was practical and possible, he would travel to Venice to seek patronage and opportunity.

Venice, the fabled city of canals. She could only imagine . . .

'For I wish to be like Barbaro,' he said, 'a man of courage and fortune who has explored and traded in the Tartary and the Peloponnese, confounded the Turks and defied the Great Horde.'

Barbaro? She did not know the name.

'A traveller,' he told her, enthusiastic now, 'a politician and military man, a merchant. Barbaro, who seeks the shine of new experiences over the dullness of old habits. As I shall do.'

She felt a scraping within; her first sense of life without Luca, that willing laugh and open delight in all that was on offer.

Her voice quavered: 'He will not let you go.'

'On the contrary,' said her brother, 'given my mediocre role in his future plans, I believe that I will travel with our father's blessing. I have already cited the disadvantages of being the second son, however I must acknowledge that there is a certain liberty as well. If our family crews a ship, then Vanni is fated to stand with our father at the helm, whereas I am the weak-minded subordinate who may wander the decks and occasionally climb the mast for a better view.'

'And me?'

'Oh, Anna, in the best cabin of course, ready to claim your riches when our ship reaches port.'

'It is not my choice,' she said acidly, 'to claim riches.'

'No,' he agreed. 'Unfortunately, as I have indicated, for each of us duty is too often the enemy of choice.'

Lengthening shadows, the world gone briefly to a blur, then came that familiar feeling, the rise of an impulse and its rapid development into an idea.

'Take me with you,' she said.

'Anna?'

'Luca, please. Take me to Venice.'

Because, what else?

Her brother touched her fingers.

'No,' he said.

'But you must,' she implored. The arguments fled her lips like arrows: this is a deal, not a marriage, and I am a profit, not a bride. The Piombinos are fools. The boy who would be my husband is inept. He is of low intellect and lower morality. I do not love him. Our mother says that I will learn to do so, but she is wrong. I will never love him. I will be trapped. I *am* trapped!

'Luca,' she said, 'I beg you. Please!'

'Sister, no.'

'But—'

'What, will you look into the well, go to the fairy city? It is make-believe, Anna.'

'You will not take me?'

‘I cannot.’

‘Then, what?’ she implored. ‘What shall I do? Oh, the second son has set his course, he takes advantage of his *certain liberty* and soars. While the first—’

‘Will be a model Florentine, as replete with riches as he is devoid of soul.’

‘Yes! Great heavens above, yes! Whereas I—’

‘Your heart,’ said Luca unexpectedly.

She stared at him, not knowing.

‘Your heart is here,’ he told her, gesturing. ‘In this place. Anna, I roam far and wide, and I have eyes. I have seen the two of you, and I have seen the direction of your heart.’

She was breathing heat, not air.

‘But to follow my heart,’ she whispered. ‘To do that?’

‘Difficult,’ he agreed. ‘Very difficult.’ Bent to the sun, they watched the dripping and layering of the universe. Luca gripped her wrist. He said, ‘Anna, outside of our father’s business plan, your heart is all that you have.’

CHAPTER 20

The summer festival was a time when landowners spoke more kindly to land-croppers, and friendship rifts with origins that had slid beyond memory were set aside, or at least temporarily ignored. Usually, Dante looked forward to the celebration. He knew that there would be people costumed as folk heroes or mighty historical figures, troupes of lively musicians and dancing; that he would watch jugglers, archers, falconers and players, and wander without bother through the lanes and alleyways as the village's families rejoiced in their day-long feasts.

However, this year, on common land near the house of Francesco da Vinci, the festival would also feature a performance from that man's precocious nephew, Leonardo, and his friend, *la scimmia*, Dante Bellomo.

It was a sultry afternoon, swifts poking holes in the air. The boys were at the land now, Leo pacing back and forth as he muttered and calculated. Behind him, an unlit torch was jammed into the crumbly soil.

'Yes,' said Leo, perhaps to himself, perhaps to the world that he assumed would always await his pronouncements. 'Yes, I think so. We will need to test, however . . .'

He swivelled and said to Dante, 'This is the spot where you will represent the angel, Raphael.'

They were going to perform the story of Tobit of Nineveh and his son Tobias. This had been Leo's idea, a shift from his first notion of presenting, symbolically, another cataclysmic event, such as a fire ripping through Milan or sections of the planet coming apart and people being plunged into hot, seething chasms. He'd justified that shift by suggesting that fires and exploding planets, although enticing as stories, did tend to imply mass death.

'Too gloomy,' he'd grinned. 'For a summer festival, anyway.'

But Dante had guessed the truth. In the past, Leo had never shirked being gloomy or confronting in his work. On the contrary, he had relished the prospect. No, this was an act of reconciliation, Leo's way of saying sorry for his thoughtlessness at the ossuary.

Did that mean a revaluing of their friendship? Dante was cautiously happy to believe so—until Leo had suggested that this time, rather than support, he should perform.

'You *must* be the angel,' Leo had told him. 'It is meant

to be and well-meant at that. Could any other mortal on God's glorious Earth be better suited to such a role?'

'Leo, I don't know. I—'

'No arguments, Dante. You are more like Raphael than Raphael is like himself.'

Nervous at the prospect, Dante had suggested that dramatically presenting such a divine figure might not be well-received.

'There will be some in the audience—'

'Who will make accusations.' Leo's annoyance had been obvious, the creative spirit stifled yet again by old, unyielding conventions. 'Unless—'

Light, he had said. Light and shadow. The angel will exist, but in a borrowed form.

'You will not *be* Raphael; you will *create* Raphael.'

'There is a difference?'

'Of course!'

A fresh, calico cloth would be erected between two stilts. The material must be pure, Leo insisted, as befitting an angel. A torch would be placed three or four *braccia* behind the cloth, with the audience seated on the other side. After the torch was lit, Dante would enter the in-between space. His shadow would be cast onto the cloth, reducing or enlarging as he moved closer to or away from the light.

'You shall wear a cloak tied at the wrists,' Leo told him. 'Lift your arms and presto! You shall have wings.' He glanced at Dante's hollowed face and added,

'I do not, of course, expect you to fly.'

Other excitements would add substance and mystery to the shadow-figure of the angel. The night breeze would make the cloth ripple. The moon's glow would offer subtle shifts in the texture of the light and moths would flit through, creating their own fleeting shadows. Moreover, the flame from the torch would enlarge and diminish as a reminder of life's transitory passage. Fittingly, while the angel was present, that flame would never die.

'But what if the wind blows out the torch?'

'It won't, Dante. Even the most fickle wind knows how to behave when in the presence of an angel.'

As the boys awaited sundown so that the shadow-play could be tested and rehearsed, Leo decided to draw the performance into his notebook.

'The first part of the story will be told in song,' he said.

'Do you have a song?'

'No, but I will write one tonight, assuming I can find my lyre. I lost it last week—or perhaps a harpy stole it? Anyway, after the song comes the blinding of Tobit. I will play Tobit and my poetry will help the audience to imagine the birds. I would use real birds, but they are skittish creatures and far too unreliable.'

'Unlike the wind.'

'Exactly.' Already Leo was sketching: a man fallen to the ground with his legs raised in agony and his hands over his eyes, three beady-eyed birds flapping towards the edge of the page.

'After this, I will change costume and become the son, Tobias, ordered by his father to collect money in Media. This will be the first appearance of the angel—you, Dante.'

More sketching.

'Having played—having *represented* the angel, you will untie your cloak and move in front of the cloth. Thus, you will become Azariah.' He dropped his chalk and flexed his hand. 'The audience will love this,' he said. 'Dante, they will love you.'

'But what do I have to say? What do I have to do?'

'Follow my instructions. Nothing could be simpler.'

As he resumed his sketching, he explained. Playing the roles of Tobias and Azariah, they would travel to Media. On the way, while they pretended to wash in the River Tigris, Leo-Tobias would describe a fish trying to swallow his foot.

'As Azariah,' he said, 'the angel in disguise, you will instruct me to catch the fish and remove its guts. Let us practise now. Go on, tell me what to do.'

'Catch the fish,' said Dante. The words came out of his mouth like flat, hard stones.

'And?'

'Remove its guts.'

'Perfect! What a fine player you are! Now, I will have the guts of a real fish concealed in my sleeve. When the time comes, with sleight of hand, I shall produce them.'

Dante felt a tiny wave of nausea.

Leo continued, 'We will then return to Nineveh, where I will use the gall from the fish to cure my father's blindness.' He finished drawing with a flourish, pocketed his chalk and closed the notebook.

Dante said, 'But you can't.'

'Can't what?'

'Cure your father's blindness.'

'Why not?'

'Because you're playing the father, Tobit, *and* the son, Tobias. Not even you can kneel alongside yourself.'

'Then it's obvious. You will have to be Tobit.'

'I can't, either. I'm already an angel and a kinsman. Leo, it's impossible.'

The problem being that word. For Leo, things might be 'not yet possible' but they were never 'impossible'.

'Allow me to reconsider,' said Leo. He lay back, folded his arms behind his head and closed his eyes.

Dante spotted her moving through the shadows cast by the trees. As she came near, he thought that Annalisa de Torriano looked older, even though it hadn't been that long since their last meeting. There was a greater fullness to her throat, he decided, and a more precise calculation behind each of her movements.

Something had happened to her.

As she left the tree line, the afternoon glare turned her into a pale, almost translucent shimmer.

Leo, who hadn't yet opened his eyes, removed a stalk from his mouth and murmured, 'O Great Bellomo, it seems that we are to be joined by the Queen of the Forest.'

Dante did not reply. Leo arose like a new plant and greeted the girl. Dante saw her expression come alive. She offered a response that he could not hear and did not even acknowledge him as Leo began to chatter merrily, then picked up and opened his notebook. Already, her stance was teetering towards over-eagerness.

This, then, was surely love. His churlish thought: the girl's squeamishness at the sight of the dead squirrel was long gone. Leo could show her the guts of a fish and she'd swoon with pleasure. A painted petal, a grinning skull, a vicious bat in a cave: anything would impress her now. She was consumed by her love for Leo, and he was . . .

What did Leo feel? As always, it was difficult to know. Did he return the girl's love? Or did he simply bask in the glossy admiration of another?

They continued to babble. Dante drifted and sat. The stink of dying plants clogged his nostrils. The sun speared pieces of coloured glass into his eyes. Exhausted by the weight of it all, he lay down and pushed his face towards the ribs of the world. Dust invaded him and became his blood. Nearby, a bee arose like a flame. The bee was small, then it was bigger, then bigger again, swelling as it came closer. He heard its angry whirr and felt the loom of its eyes and abdomen until it seemed that the bee would either kill him with its giant sting or open its mighty jaws and swallow him whole.

From elsewhere, her voice, 'I can play.'

Followed by Leo, triumphal, 'The Queen shall be Tobit!'

Dante came out of his reverie and saw that Leo and the girl were further away, near the torch.

Leo's voice again, resounding, 'The Queen shall be Sarah!'

So, she would join them to play Tobit *and* Sarah, the wife of Tobias, suddenly added to the performance. *What else*, he wondered, *would this presumptuous girl be or do in her quest for love?*

She'd catch the eye, he knew that. The dexterity in her voice, the way she could hold herself in a range of poses, the speed with which she could disassemble and reassemble her face, moving from acceptance to defiance and back again, and the freedom with which she could, at a whim, open and close the chambers of her heart: her audience—for he had no doubt that they would quickly be hers—would be enthralled.

He was sad, and angry and confused, because it was gone. The final piece of he and Leo, their shared history and—he had hoped—their future.

Annalisa de Torriano had taken it all.

He gazed at the King and the Queen as they slid elegantly towards new ambitions. How thrilled they were, how complete.

How sick his own heart.

CHAPTER 21

Ecstasy

She could not know it, of course, for no-one had such foresight, but for part of this night she would feel sumptuously alive, rather than simply living, and, within the span of her life, that time would provide an ecstasy greater than any other.

Here, at the summer festival, in the village of Vinci.

Overheated and boisterous after a day of celebrating, the crowd gathered in the field. Some complained about the thorny weeds, but Annalisa saw only perfection.

Her father, who had drunk a great deal of wine, called out, 'What is this comedy? What am I forced to see?'

No-one answered, Annalisa thinking that not many people here knew him and those who did had quickly learned to avoid conversation.

'Husband,' said Carlotta stoically, 'let us enjoy whatever is on offer.'

Annalisa was already sharp, but the presence of the

milling crowd and the smell of rain beginning its drive across the distant hills honed her further. Carefully, diplomatically, she ensured that her family sat at the front. Luca squeezed her arm, then there was a smattering of polite applause and a few rogue calls as behind the cloth, a torch flamed.

He emerged in his rose-coloured cloak like Adonis returned from the Underworld and began, as promised, with a song.

C'era un uomo fedele a Dio,
There was a man who was faithful to God,
un uomo che seppellì gli israeliti
a man who buried the Israelites
come avrebbero dovuto essere sepolti.
how they should have been buried.
Si chiamava Tobia di Ninive.
His name was Tobit of Nineveh.

For Annalisa, Leo's rich tones filled every emptiness in the universe: they replaced fallen stars, filled the drying rivers and gave breath to the sick and dying. Yet, when he finished and withdrew, and nothing more happened, there was a puzzled rumbling in the crowd, followed by calls of, 'What now?' and 'Is that it?'

Until Annalisa arose, left her family and stepped down the slope, into the light.

Did they react in any way? Call out a warning,

or move to restrain her? She could not know, for swiftly, as if born to it, she was Tobit, cowering as Leo's fanciful bird sought to blind her. She began as a frightened innocent, then screamed out her faith in God, before lifting herself to fight the unholy violence. Oh, how she fought—like a tigress, like Camilla of the Volsci!—before being terribly wounded. Rubbing her bloodied eyes and wailing at her loss of sight, Annalisa closed the scene by raising her arms in a plea for His guidance.

Thereafter, some primary force propelled her, like a gale or a tide. Quicker and more thoroughly than anyone could have expected, she became a loving father who implored his son to travel safely. Then, having hidden behind a tree while a pale-looking angel and a strutting Tobias headed to Media, she returned to the fire as the beautiful but anguished Sarah, she who would seek death rather than fall into the clutches of the demon Asmodeus.

'Lord, let not this wickedness plunder my spirit! Let me be married for love!'

Having been saved from death (and Asmodeus) by the angel—a very short scene—she became the bride of Tobias—a much longer scene!—then curved her spine and narrowed her eyes to become an older Tobit, cured by Tobias—the angel had disappeared—as evidence of God's great benevolence.

Out there, in the warm darkness, she was certain that there was prolonged cheering. Annalisa kept her smile humble as she bowed. She remained in the light and gave the audience the exquisiteness of her profile, because she was in no doubt—her performance had been magnificent.

He was furious.

They travelled without speaking. She knew there would be nothing until they were inside the villa, so she turned her eyes to the approaching storm: great lumps of rain and fire colliding like soldiers, some falling, others ignoring their wounds and renewing the battle. Thunderclaps like an axe on metal, the *contado* caught in a long, low shudder.

Vanni housed the carriage, Luca the horses. Her father marched into the villa with her mother close behind, head down, scuttling.

Like a pair of executioners, thought Annalisa. *I am being led to the noose.*

An insight as the door slammed on the whipping rain: *do what you will, for I am one who knows the truth of love, and that is my only concern.*

Despite that knowledge, once taken to the centre of the room, she felt herself to be little more than a dot in the universe.

He said, 'You have brought a grave dishonour upon me.'

Gathering her resolve, she dared to look at him. Was this her father? This scarlet bloat, this seethe of froth, hollow-eyed, dripping with wine and spit? This obscene and hairy Charon, uncombed, unclean—was this him? The man who'd had her christened as Annalisa, but who loved to call her *mio tesoro*, my treasure, who'd held her high and praised God for the gift of a daughter made in the image of her mother? Who'd led her by the hand and crooned hymns to her by starlight, and laughed at her childish jokes and pranks, who'd ordered her brothers to protect this precious stone . . .

'What stone are you, little sister? Are you a pearl?'

'Or a grimy little pebble, taken from the bottom of the Arno?'

'I am neither,' she had told them defiantly, 'for I have a ruby heart and emerald eyes and if you make me cry, I shall shed diamonds!'

'Diamond tears! How valuable you are!'

'And when you think to make yourselves rich by stealing my tears, they will vanish in your fingers and you will be sadder than I.'

She recalled her father's rollicking laughter and dismissal of his sons.

'She has more wit than either of you will ever have—go, you pair of gormless donkeys, get to work! Good-for-nothings, go!'

Was this him, this man who now looked at her so coldly?

She shivered, but was still able to say, 'Why do you stare? You know who I am.'

Her father moistened his lips and slapped her.

Shock and pain took her breath away. She heard her mother cry out and her father's bark.

'Leave her!'

Smelled his rancid fleshiness as he grappled her arms.

'Listen!' he hissed. 'Do you hear that? Pay hard attention, girl, for that is neither rain nor thunder, nothing from the natural world. No, that is the madhouse chattering of those who witnessed your little spectacle tonight. That is their mockery as they say, "Who is she?" "None other than the child of the major guildsman, Alessandro de Torriano—that's who!" "Oh, really? Well, he may be a man of wealth and status, but he is no father to allow his daughter to involve herself in such an event. What father would do that? What imbecile would do that?" Be assured that they are saying these things, so tell me, do you hear them?' He squeezed her arms and roared, 'Do you?!'

Annalisa stared at the floor, trying to will away the sting in her cheek.

'And what of tomorrow?' he asked, still upon her. 'Even here, in this stinking pit, we remain in Florence, where gossip travels faster than the plague! Oh, what a story this will make! My enemies will delight in this! Listen again so that you might hear the guild, every one of them, hiding their *florins* and walking away as they say, "How can we trust this man with our money when he cannot even control his own daughter!" How indeed?'

'And Matteo,' said Carlotta.

'Ah, yes. The contract of marriage. Listen again! That is the whole of the city talking. "This Annalisa de Torriano, isn't she betrothed to the Piombino boy?" "Well, my friends, she was, but who could know anymore?" That will become their catchphrase, you wretch of a child, "*Who could know anymore*?"'

She refused to cry, refused!

Now his hand was gripping and tilting her chin.

'Did this Bellomo, this foolish little puppy, force your participation?'

She nearly laughed.

'No!'

'Then why? Why?'

Annalisa tried to turn her face.

'Mother—'

'Child,' said Carlotta, 'do not look to me, for you have created this situation, no-one else. We have spoken before; there is nothing new for me to say.'

The words flew out.

'I will not marry him! I will not!'

'Yes, you will,' said her father roughly. The sentence was like chopped meat. 'By God and all of His most favoured instruments, you will do as I say! Now, listen to me as I tell you what shall transpire. Tomorrow, I will ride to Florence—cease your impudence and heed me, you viper! I will ride to Florence. I will visit Paolo Piombino and reassure him that any rumours of my daughter's wayward behaviour are overstated and not worthy of his consideration. Because of what you have done, I will be forced to primp like a maid—'

'Pay him,' said Carlotta. The words sliced.

'If it comes to that. More likely, I will bow down to that braying ass and say, "Dear friend, my daughter's consent is firm. She remains pious and obedient, and nothing pleases her more than the thought of marriage to your son—in fact, Paolo, as a gesture of our friendship, let us bring the date forward." Yes, girl, yes! Let you be married as quickly as possible so that your husband can take over the management of your rash and foolish temperament!'

He shoved her away and marched from the room.

Annalisa straightened and glowered. *No,* she thought, *I will not. If Luca can do as he wishes . . .*

'Mother,' she said, 'please! Let me tell you what I feel and know in my heart!'

But Carlotta's hand was raised.

'Anna,' she said, 'I have listened many times and advised on each of those occasions, but did you heed that advice? No. We ask nothing more than you follow the wishes of your parents, but you refuse to obey us.'

'Mother—'

'My own heart aches that I must say this, but here, tonight, I am ashamed that you are my daughter. I pray the situation will change in the future, but know this:

such a prayer will not be answered unless the Almighty sees that you are willing to admit your fault and tender your sorrow. If you cannot do that, may God help you, because we, your parents, will be unable to do so.'

She was quickly gone. Annalisa considered for a moment, then she walked outside and opened her face to the night so that the dark rain might cleanse the sourness from her skin.

Follow my heart, she thought, as the heavens soaked her. *Oh yes, Luca, but how?*

CHAPTER 22

Loops and Fractures

The ant continued to haul its crumb. Dante envied the insect its determination. *Brave speck*, he thought. *Faced with an enormous weight, the ant persists, whereas I . . .*

He heard the clopping of hooves, more than one horse nearing the house, then footsteps, hushed voices, his mother calling his name.

Leo stood in the main room. Amara, twisting her hands, said, 'Your friend has arrived.' She was clearly in thrall of Leo, who was a human version of the storm-scrubbed countryside, freshly painted and purified.

'O Great Bellomo, shall we walk?'

They went outside. Dante was embarrassed by the ragged lair that his parents called a garden. A few straggly herbs, an overgrown laurel and clematis gone wild like the hair of madmen; this was no garden.

No home either, not anymore.

Leo said, 'We were performing and then you were gone. I was worried about you.'

Dante felt the sun scalding his skin, the early, over-bright world already charging towards turmoil.

'I was unwell,' he said.

'I am sorry to hear that. But Dante, I saw no indication—'

'You cannot see inside me. No-one can.'

Leo's gaze settled on him like the morning light.

'Dear friend,' he said quietly, 'you must speak with him. Please.'

'You don't know what that means. No-one knows.'

'Dante, there is only one way. You must open yourself. Open your heart to your father! Of course, this will take great courage, but how else shall he know?' Ignoring Dante's protests, Leo steered him behind the laurel and said fiercely, 'A person who does not willingly climb a tree or ride a horse or swim in a forest pool—or relish the joy of performance—is a person who does not fully live! Why so? Because he worries that he will never master these or any other skills—'

'That's not true!'

'—and thus worries that he will be forever mocked by his father, which in turn leads to his mockery of himself. That is what scares him the most, this idea that he is a lesser being, when he is not. You are not!'

'I left because I was unwell!' Dante insisted.

'No, you left because you are ashamed of who you

are, which is not the person that your father wants you to be. But Dante: this is you! We cannot and should not try to alter the imprint of the soul! You are no soldier, just as—God be praised!—I will never be a notary. Dear friend, please, you must tell him this!'

'And what of you, Leo?' Dante was surprised by the surging of his own anger. *My difficult father*, he thought, *hard-tempered and bound to his past by unbreakable cords, but loving, nevertheless, in that he wants, for his son, a future with purpose.* 'What of you?' he said again. 'Your own father will not even visit you—'

'You know that he continues to grieve.'

'—let alone support your ambitions. Instead, you rely upon the goodwill of an uncle, the doting of an aunt and occasional visits to a mother who has married elsewhere . . . all of this, and yet you see fit to advise me on proper family conduct?'

For once, Leo hesitated before saying, 'Dante, I am loved.'

'As am I!' He pushed out his arms so that Leo could not come any closer. 'My parents love me in their own fashion,' he cried, 'and although it may seem paltry to you, that love is at least constant, unlike the fickle affection of others who have surely been pretending!'

There, he thought. *There!* It has been said and this moment will certainly mark the end, for Leo, charged with fickleness and pretence, will not prolong our friendship. He will go and I will go, not to live as Tobias but as my father wishes. I will travel to Florence and learn to be passably military, enough that I may take the field and place my body in the path of those who seek to interrupt the glory of the State. I will wield a meek sword and die among the brave and the less-so, before being interred as one of many who have offered themselves in sacrifice, even when they know the futility of such an act. My parents will mourn, my story will be told once, if at all, and then, as my bones bleach and crumble in the ossuary, that story will fade, just like the stories of other ordinary people who also lived modestly amid the shadows and did not, for reasons varied and uninteresting, rise above their time. *In death as in life*, he thought, *we of the multitudes are as forsaken and forgotten as the ant that hauls the crumb.*

Leo reached past his arms, held his shoulders and said, 'Dante, ride with me.'

He did, because something had freed within them, some choke or tumour. Dante took the smaller mare and held its neck as they crossed vacant hills towards the forest, the horses moving languidly over the quiet earth. They dismounted at the edge of the forest, tied the horses and walked into a glade where sunlight spun like gold coins through an ocean of air and the trees dripped green pleasures.

On the way to the cataract, they stopped to watch a porcupine. The animal's quills were wet and low.

Leo said, 'Sweet beast, why do you leave your home during daylight?' When he bent down, the porcupine sidled into a cleft between two rocks.

Nearer the cataract, the roar was extraordinary. Dante guessed that last night's rain had swelled the tributaries. He followed Leo beneath an overhang of rock and lichen, looked up and saw a furious, white passion as the water poured down and smashed onto the rocks that led, eventually, to the dark pool.

The air was cobwebbed with spray. Leo cupped his mouth and said, 'Dante, we have come this far. Will you swim?'

A shifting lattice of light, the rapid flow of the water, the world's natural generosities opening and closing like lungs . . . and now this, the offer of a moment of daring before he left for the mediocre future which was his birthright.

'Yes,' said Dante. 'I will swim.'

Watching Leo enter the pool was like watching the sun slide over the darkened brink, the brightness at its most dazzling when the great star bled along the edge of the Earth. Leo moved with his usual confidence, the water bubbling across his thighs, before he dived and vanished—then erupted like Salacia making waves as he called, 'Come on! Now, Dante. Now!'

Dante removed and folded his clothes, placed them alongside Leo's hose and sleeves, and stepped gingerly into the water. The rush of cold held him like a fever. His feet slid, but he was able to keep his balance before bending at the knees and sitting awkwardly, stomach deep. Even here, at the less turbulent end of the pool, the water ran around him in loops and fractures.

Leo glided to the centre.

'So,' he shouted, 'you are baptised!'

'I was always baptised—'

'By Nature, Dante—the only true baptism! From this time on you belong to the wilderness, as we all should.' Leo eased underwater, wiggled and shot forward, a spear of white. He resurfaced and floated next to Dante, gripping his friend's arm and anchoring them as one.

The press of cold skin. Dante shivered.

He said, 'Leo, may I just ask—'

'You may.'

He gathered his thoughts, gulped the turbulent air and said, 'Do you love her?'

'Love?' Leo looked puzzled. He released Dante's arm, flipped and sat up. 'What's this?'

'The girl,' said Dante. 'Annalisa de Torriano.'

Collisions of thunder and spray; shapes exploding and reforming. Leo shook water from his hair.

'You think I am in love with the Queen of the Forest?'

'I think that she is in love with the King, which may well be enough.'

'Dante, no.'

'No?'

'Definitely no! You are seeing a party and imagining a wedding.'

'I am seeing what she sees, and that is no party. Leo, she believes that you love her.'

'Well, I don't. I'll confess to being mindful of her wit and I have said, quite candidly, that her smile provides a worthwhile model for my art, but these are mild affections, nothing more.'

'Not to her. Have you seen how she looks at you?'

With expectations, he thought. *A lifetime's worth of them.*

Leo sighed.

He said, 'Even if I did love this girl—which I don't—the facts are plainly against marriage. Aside from the problem of me being but thirteen years of age and without means or intentions, I was born and bred in the *contado* whereas she is an out-and-out Florentine.'

'Nevertheless, she is of an age—'

'According to the convention for females, yes. And I, being male, am not. Anyway, I have it on good authority that our Queen will shortly leave the forest, because she has been promised to an ambitious young banker with that greatest of assets: profitable connections. For families like the Torrianos, little else matters.'

'On whose authority do you know this?'

'Hers,' said Leo simply. 'Come, enough of this fantasy. Let us swim.'

'But—'

'The water, Dante! The glorious water!'

He dived and arose, dived and arose, and finally he persuaded Dante to dive with him, his first time submerged. When, at the third attempt, Dante dared to open his eyes underwater, he saw a wavering world made of greens and yellows and other colours that he had never known. He saw metals and tiny jewels, and transparent coils and flashes that might equally have been water creatures or tricks of the light, and he was spellbound, for here was a beauty beyond imagination, greater than any art, or marble or dome. For a time, he was drawn to this miraculous new world and only the absence of breath could force him away, whereupon he raised himself from the water, swallowed huge containers of air and enjoyed a pleasure greater than any he had felt before.

Then Leo was with him, thrashing, exultant.

'Dante, I can't believe it!'

'What, Leo? What is it?'

'Your smile!' he cried. 'Why didn't I see this before? Your smile!'

Their streaming faces were neatly composed and framed within the stillness and antiquity of the trees. Dante saw rosy skin, the tiny lines of individuality, and he heard Leo's murmur like a single gust of wind come from beyond the clouds.

'Your smile is perfect.'

A frog cried hallelujah; a chorus followed. The boys were immersed within the silvery gifts of water and air. Their limbs were weightless, their bodies swaying to the forest's tune. When Leo's fingertips traced the dripping bow of his mouth, Dante closed his eyes to the light. As an enclosed, private moment in an achingly beautiful place, it felt like an elegant rehearsal of death.

CHAPTER 23

Dreams

What a dream, she thought. *What grace and truth—beautiful, wondrous truth!*

Awake now, she could recall every detail. They had been the only people onboard a ship that skimmed across the grey, billowing water like a migratory bird, its prow pushed forward like a beak and its sails flapping as steadily as wings. When the wind had roared, the ship had gathered pace and soared off the waves into the deepest darkness, but Annalisa had felt no fear because she was strengthened by love. Onward they'd travelled, with the stars as their guides and the planets as their friends, until finally the ship had emerged from the black and docked on an unknown shore. There, they had disembarked and walked into luminous sunshine alongside a river that she knew would never finish. As they had walked, they had sung together; a hymn that celebrated the creation of all life.

Annalisa left her bed, dressed in bland colours, tidied her face and hair, and tiptoed out to the *loggia*.

'Mother,' she said, 'I must pray.'

Carlotta was devoid of expression. The metaphor came to Annalisa: that her mother must once have been like a new work of art, filled with hopeful anticipation as she awaited her audience. But the burn of that experience, of being looked at and talked about and judged relentlessly, had, over time, rendered the painting near blank. The lines had faded to scratches and the colours had been either scrubbed away or lost beneath dust.

Her mother said, 'And the nature of this prayer?'

'Forgiveness.'

Still no expression. Carlotta's skin was hard wax.

She said, 'Go, then. Pray.'

'Shall Luca escort me?'

'Luca is busy. They are all busy. They are men.'

'Busy with what?'

'With whatever matters to them, which is certainly not the whims of an ungrateful, headstrong girl. Go.'

'Thank you, Mother. For trusting me.'

'I will not be thanked, nor do I trust you,' said Carlotta. A chill wind carried each word. As she moved indoors, she said, 'I only hope that God does, and that He is prepared to listen to you.'

There is smoke. Always.

Dear Lord, she whispered, *forgive me for my departure and help them to understand. Let them know that a ship, a journey and a song are not merely pieces of a dream, but a map for all time. Let them see past the smoke.*

She was assisted by the length of the grass behind the chapel. Crouching as low as she could, she hurried along a narrow track until she reached a line of cypress trees where she could hide and rest. Already she was dishevelled. The grass was sodden, the air like a hot, damp cloth thrown over her.

Her plan was to circumnavigate the paddocks and head towards the river. She guessed that he would be there, because he was so drawn to watercourses. If not, then she would wait for as long as she dared. The hour would come when he would arrive and once he had, they would resume what they had begun.

Because it *had* begun, she was certain of that. Her journey was underway. Whether it was God's will or the natural collisions provided by the real world, something had brought them together and that same irresistible force would ensure that they remained together—just as they had been during yesterday evening's performance.

Tobias: 'This, then, is love. All-conquering—'

Sarah: 'All-seeing!'

Tobias: 'O worthy omniscience!'

Sarah: 'Commend me to thine heart!'

Her thoughts tumbled. The King and Queen of the Royal *Palazzo* of the Forest were finished, for they were children playing children's games. Matteo Piombino and Annalisa de Torriano were also finished, for they were children being manipulated in a devious adult game. But Tobias and Sarah existed within a higher order. They were ordained to become one.

Having carefully checked her surroundings, Annalisa was about to leave the trees when she saw two riders on horseback trotting towards the forest. Even from a distance, she could see that the taller rider was Leo and the smaller one, hunchbacked as if roped to the horse, was Dante.

Who must be dismissed, she thought. Oh, she had nothing against him! Dante was an inoffensive boy, withdrawn to the point of gloominess, but his demeanour could be sweet and, as a chaperone, he was certainly useful. But there was no room. She would insist that he bid them farewell and be on his own way. He was decent enough; he'd be fine. He'd work with his father or be employed somewhere as an assistant to a higher-up assistant. Make appropriate contacts, marry a female version of himself and undertake a quiet life of service interwoven by duty. Within those necessary limitations, his prospects were perfectly reasonable.

Limited, reasonable—but such a dull fate was not for Annalisa de Torriano, and not for Leonardo da Vinci, either! Already, she could hear the voices of the future marvelling that fate had joined these two pulsating stars into a single, brilliant constellation.

Oh, Leonardo forever!

She waved as she left the trees, but she did not call out for fear of drawing too much attention to her presence, meaning that the riders did not notice her. She lost them in the outskirts of the forest and when she arrived at that same spot, the horses were tethered and feeding and the boys were gone.

To the cataract, of course! She knew that the stream would lead her there, so she followed the water's merry path, enjoying the revival of the forest in the wake of the storm. A white light had poured in like fresh milk and glossed every frond, and there was renewed pleasure in the raising of those saintly trees and the shrill psalms of the insects.

Soon enough she heard the accompanying music of the waterfall. As she quickened her pace, she mused on that sound and the contrasting sounds made by mankind. How pitiful they were: the self-important pips of rulers and drumbeats of ceremony, the monotonous hacks and thuds of industry, the whining of people at prayer. Most of all, the pathos in the voices of those who imagined that their grey and narrow love was somehow worthwhile. Whereas hers . . .

Close now. She could hear their voices slipping through the roar and was reminded of that first time: Leo romping in the water, her dismay at being discovered, the witty exchange of words and ideas that had so thrilled her, the extra thrill of being drawn into his realm. She flushed at the memories, and laughed and hurried because it was time to break through the trees and put her plan into action!

She was on the verge. The voices had either gone quiet or been suppressed by the songs of the forest. No matter. Annalisa stepped through.

Her eyes went straight to it. She saw those luxurious curls and the limp hair of the other boy, then saw how close they were in the water. She saw his hands slowly lift and take the other's face and there was an unexpected levelling of the light and silencing of the tumult, and she could not properly see what lay between them, if anything, or know the conclusion that might have come from that unseen moment—but she could imagine because she'd always been good at that, always able to conject an action in order to fill a space.

Annalisa stepped back, suddenly without form, suddenly ill, because that, surely, was what she had seen . . .

A kiss.

She turned and ran from the cataract, and as she ran, she beat back violent, virulent Nature with her arms.

A kiss.

Ran along the banks of the stream, stumbled and raised herself, ignored the twist in her knee and ran harder from the horror of having been mesmerised and fooled and nearly ruined by this devil-boy.

She ran until her heart wanted to explode and she came to the sleepy-eyed horses, still grazing. As she wheeled and spun like a crazed animal beneath the sun, her legs finally gave way, and she fell to her knees and beat the earth with flat-stick hands.

A kiss!

She stayed down, hunched over and burning from within, until a swallow came, and another. Like the other time, she remembered, her first day of exploration. She heard the birds sing their sympathies but when she lifted her face, they paused their singing and flew away.

Slowly, Annalisa unfurled. As she arose, there was an old, familiar firmness in her, a muscularity that she recognised as the prelude to cold, precise anger.

Who am I? None other than the child of the major guildsman, Alessandro de Torriano.

She knew now that her dream had been both illusion and warning. Beneath any kiss, the predator's bite awaited.

Annalisa went to the larger of the two horses and stroked its flank. The horse murmured appreciatively. She stroked again, then leaned down, reached beneath the saddle and loosened the strap. Not a lot, but enough that an arrogant rider would deservedly look like a fool.

Did the sun bow? *It may have done*, she thought, *for I am a Torriano and we are from Florence. You dare to cause us pain and we will return the favour, with interest.*

That is the Torriano way, the Florentine way.

Swiftly, looking only to the path ahead, Annalisa rushed home through the long grass.

CHAPTER 24

Climbing and Falling

They were dried and dressed, sitting away from the noise. A single sunbeam had strayed from the pack and fallen like beeswax between them.

Dante said, 'What will you do?' From this point on, he meant. Tomorrow, the day after, the day after that. The next month and year, more years, moving into adulthood and that part of a person's life when hope and vision might align and lead to greater wisdom.

He added, quite mildly, 'You speak of my future, but what of your own?'

'I will learn,' said Leo. His eyes were hooded and he sounded sleepy.

'Learn what?'

This time Leo laughed and it was a breeze, light and disconnected.

'I don't know yet,' he said. 'Isn't that the point?'

Around them the plants flourished, their leaves broadening to catch the moisture, their buds unravelling to release brilliant, flame-shaped petals. Leo perched forward.

He said, 'My father has sent me a letter. He tells me that he is preparing my way.'

A notary, he explained, served many powerful clients. Ser Piero had access to all sectors of the guild, to the merchants and doctors and tradesmen, but also, tellingly, to the artists.

'He says that when the timing is right, he will speak with Andrea del Verrocchio.'

'Leo! To work with Verrocchio—'

'An opportunity, yes. We will see. My father's promises are always well-intended, however . . .'

He left the sentence unfinished. Across the pool, the waterfall shattered and sprayed. Verrocchio or not, said Leo, his future was hard to predict because there was so much to know. And who could properly organise their learning when the advancement of knowledge hurtled as it did, outpacing even the hours and days?

'I must learn well,' he insisted. 'Truths over possibilities. Too many ideas exist for *their* time, not *all* time.' His grin seemed apologetic. 'You ask me what I will do. Dear friend, it is difficult to say for I have a million plans. Probably more than a million! This is why, too often, I begin a project but I cannot end, because I am taken by something else, another thought or plan, and over there, another. It is selfish, I know, and clearly futile, but I wish for many lives, for how else will I learn what I need to know?'

'You will be famous,' Dante told him.

'Perhaps, perhaps not. It does not matter. Fame is a fanciful notion, invented by idiots and supported by idlers. God never appointed fame. Like Him, I do not care for any of that.'

'What, then? What do you care for?'

'A better way,' said Leo slowly. 'There must always be a better way.'

Because he was a seeker, thought Dante. *The one at the front.* Throughout Leo's life, people would scoff at what he said and did. Some would follow, but most would remain to the side, oblivious, until the chance came to step in and enjoy the benefits of his work. Such were the mechanics of the world.

He said, 'You will find many better ways because you can do anything.'

Leo squeezed his arm, before replying in a brighter voice, 'No-one can do anything, Dante. I can, however, attempt to draw your perfect smile. That is the worthiest of tasks, so let me begin.'

He worked with great care. When he had finished and tucked away his notebook—without showing Dante because, he claimed, the sketch was not yet good enough—they left the cataract, Leo gesturing that Dante should lead the way. Feeling encouraged by his first swim, he was pleased to do so.

They walked along, chattering about types of clouds and the flight paths of butterflies, until Dante said, 'Leo, if I am not to be a soldier—'

'Dante, please. Whatever the future holds, you must not do that.'

'Then what?'

Because, he thought, *I must have sound reasons for challenging my father's decision. I must be able to say, with great conviction, 'Father, I respect your wishes, however I hope to—', or 'I believe that I am better suited to—'.*

With Stefano, as with most Florentine fathers, open defiance would never work.

They stopped near the convergence of the forest and the meadows. Ahead, Dante could see what remained of the day, prisms of light hanging like lanterns between the trees.

'Tell me,' he said. 'Please, Leo. Tell me what I should do?'

'What you must do, who you might become . . . Dante, the answers to these questions are obvious.'

'Not to me.'

'Goodness lives in your soul.' Leo was tapping a tree at different points, listening for variations in the sound. 'You are cleaner than the sky. Although you can be unkind to yourself, your kindness to others is beyond reproach. Most of all, you want to love. No, more than that. You want to love *all*.'

He stopped tapping and faced Dante.

'My dear friend,' he said, 'you are God's best type of citizen.'

'I am?'

'You are. And that is why you must join the clergy.'

Dante stared at Leo, then shook his head.

'No.'

'Why not? Dante, tell me, why not?'

'My father says they are corrupt.'

'Your father is correct. Some of the greatest sinners in Florence—across Italy, no doubt; probably all of Europe—are priests. They treat their sacred vows like underclothes that may be soiled and washed and re-soiled and re-washed, and on it goes. Uncle Francesco says that the one reliable truth about churchmen is that they will always opt for a pay-off over a prayer.'

'Then—'

'It is *because* they are corrupt that you must join them. You have faith, do you not?'

'Of course.'

'Moreover, you are genuinely virtuous. Dante, renewal might begin with a leader, but it can only persist if there are good people who are prepared to stand firm behind that leader. You are one of those.'

'The priesthood?' He could scarcely believe the idea and yet, there was a warmth . . .

Leo gripped his wrists.

'We are all born to serve,' he said. 'For some, that

means the battlefield. For others, the council or the guild, the anvil, the workshop, the ship, the university. But you, my pure-hearted friend, make no mistake: you were born for the church. You were born to serve God.'

And now, Dante thought, *you have made me strong.*

The horses snorted and nuzzled. Dante stroked their noses and looked into their trusting eyes and the idea came: he would ride the bigger mare. *Ride her home*, he thought. *Show my father that I have determination and courage enough to overcome any adversity. Show him how I can serve Florence and the world in ways that he hasn't considered.*

He suggested his plan.

Leo grinned and said, 'See how your baptism has created the new you?'

But when Dante tried to mount, the stirrup was too high, the horse's back beyond his leap.

'Let me raise you.'

Not this time. Dante had another idea. Under his instruction—his!—Leo guided the mare beneath a tree and held her there. Using a staircase of lower branches, Dante climbed the tree. Ignoring the nausea in his stomach and the weakness of his limbs, he edged along a branch until he was above the horse, then gripped the branch, lowered himself and dropped onto the saddle, which gave a little but held.

'Bravo!' Leo led the horse back into the open. 'Soon you will ride like the Anemoi!'

While Leo mounted the smaller mare and adjusted the reins, Dante gazed at the golden span of the *contado*. He hadn't properly noticed it before, but there was a simple beauty in the pleats and rolls of the fields. That same beauty came in the merging of heat, light, air and soil, and in the jumble and kiss of colours that fell from the heavens and lifted from the earth.

I am of this world, he thought, and welcomed that new gladness into his heart.

Leo was ready. They dug their heels and urged the horses into a trot. Dante quickly felt the power of the larger mare, her joint muscles beginning to ripple as she moved into her work. He was not quite steady, but that was to be expected, he thought, because of the size of the horse. Besides, he was riding towards the future and there would always be times of unsteadiness, just as there would always be the calming advent of a new day.

They crossed a spongey plateau and rode towards a crest, after which the land dipped into a field formed of plough-gouges and stubble. Sunlight striking the crest shot arrows of gold skyward. Dante's horse was moving quickly now, relishing the gallop, so he tightened his hold. Beyond the thundering staccato of the hooves, he could hear Leo whooping. That noise seemed to further spur the mare. Dante tried to slow her, but the horse raced on and they hit the crest hard. He felt her body lurch as they hurtled into the dip, then heave as she tried to correct, and suddenly he was aware of danger, the saddle sliding, the reins slipping away from his fists, the countryside coming to claim him.

Thereafter, it happened with inevitability and was the sum of all falls; he was Eutychus leaving the window, Icarus tumbling from the sky. The beautiful world spun out of control. A cry gripped and un-gripped his heart, then he was free of it all, arcing and weightless, lost in time. He was Phaethon, too light for his father's chariot and too weak for his rampaging horses; Phaethon, thrown aloft, struck by lightning and falling; Phaethon, plunging without stopping into the sea, where the cold black welcomed and enfolded him.

CHAPTER 25

Exodus

Her *matrimonium* took place on a dark and turbulent day in August. Matteo agreed to love, honour and protect her, and Annalisa agreed that she would obey him. The notary, a swarthy but kind-looking man, was extraordinarily careful in taking her right hand and she wondered if that hand was already deemed to have a value, like a precious metal or cloth.

She listened to the priest's intonations and swallowed her own bile. As rain lashed the cathedral, the rings were blessed and exchanged and the families gave each other gifts.

The banquet was lavish. Her father had commissioned a sculpture made entirely from sugar, Hymen topped by a wreath of flowers and holding a torch. Paolo Piombino insisted on kissing her cheeks, frequently. His kisses were long and wet.

Vanni guzzled a large cup of wine and said to her,

'You will rise in society, sister. The Piombinos are much favoured by the Medici family.'

He stared at her for a moment and Annalisa stared back, but she did not smile.

She endured the *nozze*, during which she was paraded towards the Piombino house. The storm had cleared so there were plenty of observers lining the streets, their faces lit ruby by the heat of the night and strategically placed flames.

'They are eager,' said Matteo, one of the few times that he had spoken to her.

No, she thought miserably, *they are leering drunks and I am a bride who feels like the seller's bird, tethered to a perch in a cage.*

They arrived at the front gate. Luca held her close for a moment and whispered that tomorrow he would travel to Venice.

'With our father's blessing?' she asked, and he refused to answer or look at her. A moment of separation, before—

'Pray for me?' he asked.

'If you'll pray for me,' she told him. Somehow, she restrained her tears.

Her mother manufactured an appearance of joy with her usual expertise. Her father was bloated with drink and self-importance. Annalisa and Matteo were escorted through the gate. They entered the house to the rousing cheers of the crowd, and the remainder of the evening occurred as Carlotta had suggested it would.

Over a year had passed when she was stunned to find him in the city. She had heard nothing and had even managed to put her treachery with the saddle-strap out of her mind when, crossing a *piazza*, the weight of her unborn child straining her lower back, she spotted Leo, sitting against the wheel of a cart. He was drawing in his notebook. She saw that he was longer and leaner, and those unruly curls had been tugged into a manageable bundle, but the mannerisms were unchanged: legs splayed, head angled close to the page, left hand making quick backward strokes of the pencil. She stood aside so that others might pass and gazed for a moment, wondering if she dared—

Leo looked up. Was she a beacon? Did she send a light or message? Perhaps so, for his eyes were instantly upon her.

Annalisa flushed, but she could not move and did not want to move, as Leo closed his notebook, stood and walked in her direction. She was surprised to see that there was little vigour in his gait, nor did he offer anything more than acknowledgement as he stood before her.

'You are married,' he said.

She nodded, keeping her palms across her swollen belly.

'And what of you?' she asked, for she did not want to discuss marriage or children, any of that. 'What brings you to Florence?'

'Verrocchio's workshop,' he told her. 'I am apprenticed.'

'Congratulations. Your dreams will be fulfilled.'

He inclined his head politely, but said, 'Dreams mean nothing. I will learn and that will be enough.'

How strange, she thought, *that there is only emptiness between us: the soaring ship and eternal river, the love-hymn of Tobias and Sarah, all of it evaporated like . . . like smoke.*

She said flatly, 'Do you enjoy our city?'

'No,' he told her, 'for I belong among plants, not stones. However, for now, this is what I must do.'

'And what of your home?' she asked, but indifferently. She had spent the most recent summer at the luxurious and flamboyant Piombino estate, much bigger and more bearable than the Torriano villa and that tedious little village.

'Vinci is not the same,' he said, 'and it will never be the same again.'

She detected a great sorrow sitting like water beneath his words.

'How so?'

Leo said, 'There is no Dante.'

No Dante? The question must have been written all over her features, for he answered with slow, terrible factuality.

'You have not heard? The day after our harvest festival performance, we went riding. As a demonstration of his new courage, Dante insisted on taking the larger horse. The saddle slipped. He was badly injured.'

Annalisa, feeling light-headed, placed her hand against a wall. The stone was cool and hard.

'He was flung to the ground,' Leo told her. 'I was just behind him when it happened. His head struck a rock. At first, I thought he was killed. Perhaps . . .' He grimaced and said in a low voice, 'The bone has healed, the skin too. But his mind is broken.'

A sickness spread through each part of her.

She managed to say, 'Where is he?'

Leo named the place, an asylum on the outskirts of the city.

'His parents are distraught,' he said. 'They tried, but they could not keep him at home. It was too distressing for them.'

He left her then, because they both understood that there was nothing more to say; *as if,* she thought sadly, *that small, delicate boy really had been the angel who might have blessed their togetherness.*

Now Leo was gone from her, she assumed for all time. The *piazza* was in uproar as a disagreement threatened to becomc a fight. Annalisa gagged on air that tasted of brass and smoke. She lumbered to the cathedral and prayed, lumbered home and lay in a darkened room. For once, the baby was quiet, but there was a blood-stained rock also positioned inside Annalisa, and she knew that, unlike her unborn child, that rock would never leave her.

October turned cold so she was able to wear a hood and scarf to disguise and protect herself. Seen from the outside, the asylum was like a prison: high stone walls and a single, heavy door. Once admitted, she was taken down a long corridor by a silent attendant. Their footsteps echoed and she felt trepidation pricking the back of her neck.

Inside a freezing office, a doctor awaited her. He did not introduce himself.

Instead, he said, 'You wish to see one of our patients. Are you family?'

'His cousin.'

The doctor pondered for a moment. His face was a mask.

'Very well,' he said. 'Come with me.'

More corridors. The walls wept years of pain and sounds emerged like ghosts: shouts and cries, a low moan. The doctor walked briskly.

He said, 'We are a hospital, but those patients with illnesses of the brain are for the most part incurable. We can give them dignity and pray for their eternal salvation, but little else can be done.'

They came to a door. The doctor produced a key, unlocked the door and swung it open. Inside the room, a single candle burned. Annalisa smelled staleness and damp. As her eyes adjusted to the weak light, she saw the outlines of people laying on cots. The people were unmoving.

The doctor handed her the candle and pointed to a cot next to a wall. Annalisa stepped closer. Fear beat its wings against her lungs. She saw Dante on his back, beneath a blanket. He was very thin and there was a cloth tied around his crown, but the prettiness of his face was unaltered, as if cast in marble.

When she saw that his eyes were open, she said instinctively, 'Dante, it's me, it's the Queen,' but then she realised that those eyes were empty, wastelands replacing meadows.

She whispered to the doctor, 'Is he even alive?'

'For now,' the doctor told her. 'There is yearning enough in his body and soul that he will accept some soup and water. In time, perhaps a year, probably less, these meagre quantities will not be sufficient. But, for now, his heart flutters and his blood moves.'

'But his mind—'

'His mind is elsewhere.'

She had to ask. 'Will it ever return?'

'No,' said the doctor. He exhaled slowly. 'A cruel fate,' he said. 'Perhaps, the cruellest.' He paused, then added, 'I have been told that, prior to his accident, this young man led a most virtuous life. As a doctor, I have always thought it both a curiosity and a sadness that, more often than not, the roses in our world are cut early, while the weeds survive.' He took the candle, then gestured Annalisa towards the door.

'Some advice,' he said. 'You are with child. That is

the future that you must consider. Your friend . . . your cousin is safe here, but understand, he will not recover and nothing more can be done.'

She began the remainder of her life in a haze that never left—*as if*, she sometimes thought, *I am stuck forever in that candle-lit room, not as a real person, but as a shadow thrown onto a surface.*

Like her mother, she had three children, but the third, her only boy, was weak-minded and miserable and she knew that God had not forgotten—she was being punished for her sin in the *contado*. There were other punishments too: the fatal eruption of her father's heart after a gluttonous celebration at the Guild, and the mystery of Luca's disappearance, the latter culminating in Vanni's long search and eventual discovery that their beloved brother had been murdered by Ottoman invaders during a siege at the Venetian stronghold of Scutari.

Within Annalisa's more immediate realm, her husband's success was never as acute as expected, nor did his hands remain tender, especially after drink. She quietly confirmed that there were others with whom he sought fulfilment and, in so doing, proved that her mother's definition of love was wrong, had always been wrong. There would never be love between her and Matteo, not even an affection or familiarity which could be passed off as steady and reliable. Instead, she thought, there was a chasm—or perhaps their marriage was like a pool beneath a cataract, left waterless after a long drought.

As her body calcified and she aged towards loneliness, Annalisa's only sustenance was her memories of a glorious summer exploring the *contado* and jousting with the King of the Forest. When those memories became too painful to bear, she took to kneeling every day on the cold, hard floor of the Cathedral of Santa Maria del Fiore. Until Carlotta's death, aged sixty, at the hands of the pestilence, Annalisa was often accompanied by her mother. The two women prayed silently and lit candles together, although neither would say why or for whom.

Epilogue

1st May 1519: Amboise, France
Main bedroom, Château de Cloux

Auguste, having seen that the door was ajar, had entered tentatively. The master, who was a long-term guest of the king, had lately been unwell: his skin turned as pale as cheese and his wavy hair gone straight and lank. These days, that once formidable voice cracked and wheezed, and the mischievous glint in his eyes was too often reduced to the tarnish of old metal.

At the age of twelve, Auguste was not afraid of the master, who was invariably kind, but he was afraid of illness. His mother, Mathurine, however, had been unsympathetic.

'He's an old man,' she'd said, 'and old age is not contagious. Now, go upstairs and ask him if he'd like some soup. That's what he needs. A big bowl of warm onion soup and a long rest. That's all any of us needs.'

Auguste had long ago learned the futility of arguing with his mother, especially when it came to advice on good health being linked to onion soup. He went upstairs.

The room was magnificent. The shutters on the largest window had been pinned back to let in the tawny light that arose from the valley. That light fell gently on a writing table and a chair. There was a fireplace with logs still smouldering, despite the lateness of the season, but the main feature of the room was the bed, with its carved canopy and spiral pillars, red brocade curtains and those golden ropes used to tie back the curtains in the master's favoured, complex knots.

The old man lay on this bed, apparently asleep.

Auguste waited near the doorway, but the master's breathing was deep. Wondering what he should do, he looked around the room and saw that a notebook had been left open on the writing table.

A window to the master's ideas. *Should I?* he thought. What if the old man awoke suddenly? Or if Auguste's mother came up the steps, or worse, Battista?

Early afternoon: the chateau seemed quiet. Auguste steeled himself, crept over to the table and gazed at the open pages. He saw four triangles drawn on the right side. There were different sized rectangles inside each triangle, with obscure numbers jotted onto the margins in the master's backward writing. Who knew what it all meant? Certainly not Auguste, who, as the son of a cook, had not been entitled to any schooling. Besides, his mother had told him many times, 'The master is the guest of our most royal lord. That is our only concern.'

But Auguste, a curious child, wanted to know more.

Gathering courage, he tiptoed further into the bedroom. Three of the master's paintings had been placed against a wall: a lady, a man, and two ladies holding a little boy, who was playing with a lamb. Auguste bent down to look more closely at the paintings. He liked the little boy's gentle, loving features, and he liked the man too, who looked like an older version of the boy, but he found the lady to be the most mesmerising. What was inside her mind?

He was still looking, lost in a reverie, when a noise startled him. Auguste sprang up and turned to see the imposing bulk of the master's personal servant framed within the doorway.

'Auguste? What are you doing?'

'I'm sorry,' stammered the boy. 'I didn't mean—'

'Were you snooping? Is that it?'

'No, I came to see if the master would like some onion soup! My mother says—'

'You can't just walk in here,' said Battista de Vilanis coldly. 'The master is unwell. He needs his rest and he certainly doesn't need to be disturbed by the likes of you. Now, off you go!'

'Oh, leave him,' crackled a voice from the bed. 'He's a boy, he's curious.'

They looked across and saw that the master had somehow, silently, raised himself to a sitting position.

'He has no right to be here,' Battista whined, but the master simply raised his misshapen finger to his lips.

Battista was silent. The master nodded.

'Auguste,' he said. 'Come closer.'

His action in removing his covers had let loose a smell of sickness that permeated the still, smoky air. As Auguste approached, he was more nervous than ever. But the master smiled encouragingly, then patted Auguste's arm with an uncle's affection.

'You like my paintings?'

'Yes.'

'You probably like them more than I do.' The master sighed. 'Year after year of toil, but never perfect. What do you think, Auguste? You and I are humans, not gods. Can we ever achieve perfection?'

'Master,' said the boy, 'I believe . . .'

'Yes? Go on, don't be shy. Out with it.'

'I believe that you have already achieved perfection.'

'Oh, I have? Did you hear that, Battista? Youth has spoken, perfection is mine!'

'Congratulations, Master.'

'Tell me,' said the old man to Auguste, 'how have I done this?'

The boy pointed to the wall.

'The lady,' he said.

'Ah, yes. *La Gioconda*. Begun too many years ago as yet another favour to my father. Auguste, I have spent much of my life doing favours for people. Is that a good thing? For them, yes. For me, I'm not so sure. Anyway, bring her to me.'

'Master, is that wise?'

'Battista, please. Do not fuss. This boy belongs to a woman who wields knives for a living. He knows the benefits of being careful. Auguste, quickly, before I die.'

'Master!'

'A joke, Battista! How jumpy you are today! Come, boy. The painting.'

Auguste did as he was asked. Holding the lady felt like undertaking the Eucharist, when he was instructed to swallow the body and blood of Christ. His fingers warmed and he felt his own blood race through his scrappy body.

The old man grasped the wooden panel in his wrinkly hands, surveyed the painting for a moment, then turned it around.

'Tell me, Auguste, what do you see?'

'A lady, Master.'

'Yes, but what do you see *within?* What are these perfections that you claim?'

'I think—it is the colours, Master, and the lines, they are . . .'

When the words would not come, Battista interrupted, saying, '*Sfumato*, boy. The master is the genius who created this technique.'

'Blurring and mellowing,' said the old man. His tone had softened.

'As if we are looking through smoke,' whispered the boy.

'Exactly, Auguste. Do you know why I paint in this way?'

'Master, I cannot—'

'Because no matter how closely we might examine our remarkable world, nothing is ever as it seems.'

'Looking through smoke? Is that what he said?' Battista was becoming impatient. 'Not a bad analogy, I suppose, but that will do, boy. It is time for you to go.'

But the master waved away Battista's prattle.

'The painting,' he said. 'Anything else?'

Auguste hesitated, then said, very earnestly, 'The lady is beautiful.'

'She is.'

'She watches me.'

'That is good. She watches me also. She watches the watchers! So, it is her face and her eyes? These are also perfections?'

'Her face, her eyes and everything else,' said Auguste in a rush, 'but mostly, Master, it is her mouth. You have given her a secret. I like that.'

'Oh, you do?'

'Yes. It is a secret that no-one will ever know,' he said. 'And that is why she is perfect. Because she . . . because . . .'

The words? The words!

'Because she smiles, Master, and yet behind that smile

she has a secret. So, she is neither happy nor sad. She is just . . . secretive. And that is how people are, I think.'

The master was silent. Auguste wondered if he was in a dream: the body and the blood, rushing and rising. Even so, he could not stop himself from reaching in and tracing the shape of the lady's lips with his finger.

'Her smile is perfect,' he whispered.

'It is not *her* smile,' said the old man, staring down at the panel. 'It is his.'

A dove alighted on the windowsill. Auguste, unsure of what the master meant, glanced at Battista, whose expression made his own view clear: *he is old, he says these things, they are not always . . . He is not always . . .*

They both watched as the master placed the panel face-down on the bed and wiped his eyes. Suddenly, he seemed tired again.

'Auguste,' he rasped, 'please thank your mother for her kindness, but I will not be taking soup today.'

The boy nodded and scurried out the door, nearly tripping on the steps as he returned to the kitchen.

Battista de Vilanis picked up the painting and straightened the coverlet on the bed.

He said, 'That is a strange lad,' and the old man shrugged.

'No, he is interested in the whole of life, not just those parts that affect him. Is that not a good quality for a boy to have? For anyone to have?'

Battista chose not to reply.

He returned *La Gioconda* to her place against the wall, then he said, 'The smile is bewitching. Master, was the boy correct? Does the lady have a secret?'

The old man coughed hard, before settling back into his pillows and closing his eyes.

'Yes,' he said. 'I believe she does.'

Author's Note

When I was in primary school, our classwork included monthly projects. Back then, doing a project meant picking a topic, buying a large piece of cartridge paper from the newsagency and filling it with notes, drawings, maps and timelines—all handwritten and hand-drawn, of course. There were no computers or digital devices to ease the workload.

I can't remember how old I was—probably around ten or eleven—but I do know that I created a project on Leonardo da Vinci. I was fascinated by the scope and diversity of his talents, and have remained that way ever since. Later on, studying history at university, I found out more about the Renaissance period and that also became a fascination. I loved the bold characters, incredible achievements and endless intrigue. It was inevitable that, eventually, I would write a story set into this period.

Although this is a work of fiction, I have tried to stay true to its historical background. That said, for storytelling purposes, I have made certain choices regarding the timeline of Leonardo's adolescence. For example, there is uncertainty among historians as to the year in which he began his apprenticeship with

Verrocchio; I have chosen 1466, the 'late' option, to allow him to be older. Although it is probable that he left Vinci in 1464 to live with his father in Florence, I have resisted that probability, again to allow Leonardo to be older and potentially more mature during the summer in which this story unfolds.

In a similar vein, I have remoulded the landscape to better fit the narrative, pushing the river closer to the village and inventing a forest with a cataract so as to explore his fascination with water. I have also reimagined and used some recorded incidents from different stages of Leonardo's life, for example his discovery of a fossil in a cave, his use of apple cores to measure the currents of a river, his studies of dead bodies, his creation of a terrifying plaque on commission, and the tale about a kite attacking his mouth when he was a baby. In doing all of these things, I can only hope that my fiction remains true to the spirit of this remarkable man, and especially to his creed of boundless curiosity and open humanity.

While Dante Bellomo is an imagined figure (as are the Torriano and Piombino families), it is true that da Vinci did maintain very close friendships with young men throughout his life. Most notable of these were Gian Giacomo Caprotti, an opportunist whom da Vinci called Salai, meaning 'little devil', and the more devoted, gentler Francesco Melzi. The sixteenth century biographer Giorgio Vasari noted that Melzi 'was a very beautiful boy, and much beloved by him'. Dante has been created and written with this person in mind.

A note on the biblical story of Tobit of Nineveh: in Europe at this time, people looked to this story as a source of comfort before travel. The Age of Discovery had begun and, like most Italian city-states, Florence was keen to take advantage of the opening-up of trade routes and explore the possibility of empire-building. People with entrepreneurial spirit were intent on seeking adventure and experiences beyond their local areas. In so doing, they hoped to be guided and protected by St Raphael, the patron saint of travel, as happened with Tobias in the story.

I consulted many sources in preparing and writing *Leonardo Forever*, but am particularly indebted to the scholarship of Walter Isaacson, as seen in his wide-ranging, highly detailed and thoughtful biography, *Leonardo da Vinci*.

Da Vinci died on the day after that used for my epilogue, on 2 May 1519. His legacy has informed the world ever since, and continues to do so.

THE STORY OF TOBIT AND TOBIAS (from *The Book of Tobit*)

Tobit of Nineveh was imprisoned by Salmanazar, king of the Assyrians, and then by Sennacherib, the king's cruel son. Despite his grim situation, Tobit remained committed to a Christian way of life. 'He fed the hungry, and gave clothes to the naked, and was careful to bury the dead' (1:20).

The act of burial in the story refers to the bodies of Israelites who had been killed by the Assyrians. Tobit was not allowed to do this, so, to avoid detection, he completed the burials at night. However, misfortune fell upon him. 'As he was sleeping, hot dung out of a swallow's nest fell upon his eyes, and he was made blind' (2:11).

Tobit survived, and he and his wife Anna had a son, Tobias. When Tobias was old enough, his father asked him to go to Media (an ancient country in the north-west of Iran) to recover 'ten talents of silver' (4:21) from a man named Gabelus. Meanwhile, in Media, Sarah, the daughter of Raguel, was praying to God because she had been 'given to seven husbands' (3:8) and a devil named Asmodeus had killed them all, one by one, so she could never be properly married.

Before he left, Tobias met 'a beautiful young man' (5:5) who knew the way to Media. The young man, who said his name was Azarias, promised Tobit that he would guide Tobias on his journey. Anna was worried about Tobias's safety, but Tobit was convinced that Azarias was an angel, sent by God, and that Tobias would therefore be safe.

Tobias and Azarias headed for Media. On the way, Tobias decided to wash his feet in the river Tigris and was attacked by a huge fish. Azarias, who was indeed an angel, helped Tobias to defeat the fish, then advised him to 'take out the entrails of the fish, and lay up his heart, and his gall, and his liver for thee: for these are necessary for useful medicines' (6:5).

When they reached Media, Azarias told Tobias to seek Sarah's hand in marriage. Tobias was wary, because he'd heard of the troubles with Asmodeus, but Azarias told him not to worry because he could defeat Asmodeus by placing 'the liver of the fish on the fire, and the devil shall be driven away' (6:19). Raguel, who knew that Tobias was 'the son of a good and most virtuous man' (7:7), was happy for him to marry Sarah, but he too was concerned about the interference of Asmodeus. However, Azarias convinced Raguel that God was on their side and a wedding feast was prepared.

At the feast, Tobias followed the angel's advice and placed the fish's liver over hot coals. The smoke that came from the coals broke the devil's curse and Asmodeus was defeated. The family rejoiced and Raguel accepted Tobias as Sarah's husband. Tobias asked Gabelus to come to the wedding and duly received the silver that his father was owed.

Back in Nineveh, Tobit and Anna did not know of Tobias's happiness, because he hadn't returned home when he was supposed to. Anna wept for her son, asking, 'Why did we send thee to go to a strange country, the light of our eyes, the staff of our old age, the comfort of our life, the hope of our posterity?' (10:4).

In Media, Raguel agreed that Tobias should return home and that Sarah should travel with him. However, Azarias suggested that he and Tobias should go ahead of Sarah, and that Tobias 'take with thee of the gall of the fish, for it will be necessary' (11:4). Tobias did this and was greeted by his overjoyed parents. Following the angel's instructions, he took the fish's gall and used it as an ointment on his father's eyes, after which a miracle happened: 'A white skin began to come out of his eyes, like the skin of an egg . . . And Tobias took hold of it, and drew it from his eyes, and immediately he recovered his sight' (11:14-15).

Tobit was no longer blind. As the family celebrated,

Azarias revealed his identity as an angel who had been sent by God, but 'it is time therefore that I return to Him that sent me' (12:20).

The family's Christian faith had been reinforced by all that had happened. Tobit 'lived two and forty years [more] and saw the children of his grandchildren. And after he had lived a hundred and two years, he was buried honourably in Nineveh' (14:1-2).

Glossary

Adonis In Greek mythology: a beautiful mortal, or human, who was raised in the Underworld and returned to Earth as a beautiful young man.

Aeneid An epic poem, written by Virgil, which follows the traveller Aeneas as he goes from Troy to Italy, and details the war between the Trojans and the Italians.

Anemoi In Greek mythology: the wind gods, often shown as horses. They travelled north, south, east or west and were linked to the seasons.

Andrea del Verrocchio 1435–1488. Florentine painter, sculptor and goldsmith who ran the workshop where da Vinci was apprenticed and trained.

Andrea Orcagna 1308–1368. Florentine artist and architect from a prominent family, best known for his work in various churches.

Anghiari	Site of a battle in 1440 between Florence and Milan, won by Florence. Da Vinci painted a scene from the battle in 1505, however the painting was lost.
Antaeus	In Greek mythology: a giant who was defeated by Hercules as part of the Twelve Labours.
Apollo	In Greek mythology: a god, regarded as the ideal in terms of beauty and youth.
Arno	A river that runs through the Italian region known as Tuscany, including the city of Florence.
Bacchus	In Roman mythology: the god of wine, fertility and theatre.
Boccaccio	A highly influential Italian writer and poet, best known for a book of short stories called *The Decameron*.
Book of Hours	A Christian manuscript containing prayers, texts and psalms.

Byzantium An ancient Greek colony, now Istanbul, the capital of Turkey.

Camilla of the Volsci A warrior princess from Virgil's *Aeneid,* known for her running speed.

Cathedral of Santa Maria del Fiore Florence's main cathedral, begun as a Gothic building in 1296 and finished in 1436 with the famous dome designed by Filippo Brunelleschi.

Ceres In Roman mythology: the goddess of agriculture and fertility. Ceres was also acknowledged during marriages and funerals.

Charon In Greek mythology: the ferryman who carried the souls of the dead across the river Styx and into the Underworld.

Eutychus From Chapter 20 of Acts in the New Testament: Eutychus sleeps while listening to a sermon, falls out a window and seems to die. However, St Paul believes he is alive and carries him back upstairs.

Filippo Brunelleschi 1377–1446. Architect, designer and engineer who built the famous dome on Florence's main cathedral and developed the principle of linear perspective.

Fra (Father) Angelico 1395–1455. A Dominican friar who painted a series of brilliant frescos. He was made a saint by the Catholic church in 1982.

Giosafat Barbaro 1413–1494. Traveller and trader who spent a lot of time in places that we now know as Greece, Russia and the Middle East.

Giotto di Bondone 1266–1337. A painter whose innovative work began the style of art that became known as the Renaissance.

Great Horde Refers to the Mongol Empire of Central Asia.

Hercules In Greek mythology: the son of Zeus who famously took on a range of challenges, the Twelve Labours.

He was worshipped in Florence as a symbol of power.

Hymen	In Greek and Roman mythology: the god of marriage.
Icarus	In Greek mythology: Icarus attempted to escape from Crete by flying with wings made of feathers and wax. However, he flew too close to the sun, the wax melted and Icarus fell to his death.
Jephthah	In the Bible's Book of Judges, Jephthah, having led the Israelites to victory in battle, vowed to sacrifice to God whatever first came out of the door of his house. Unfortunately, it was his daughter.
John the Baptist	A preacher and prophet, revered in many religious faiths.
Jupiter	In Roman mythology: the god of the sky, also king of the gods. Zeus was his equivalent in Ancient Greek mythology.

La Gioconda Da Vinci's most famous painting, widely known as the *Mona Lisa,* now on display at the Louvre Museum in Paris.

Leviathan An enormous, mythical seamonster.

Luke *The Gospel of Luke* in the Bible's New Testament tells the story of Jesus.

Marco Polo 1254–1324. Famous for travelling to the Far East and opening up the Silk Road, he inspired other travellers such as Christopher Columbus, the discoverer of America.

Masaccio 1401–1428. During his brief but brilliant life, Masaccio shifted Italian painting from Gothic to a more natural, humanist style.

Medici Family The House of Medici was a powerful banking dynasty that ruled the Republic of Florence for centuries and produced several Italian popes.

Milan	Northern Italian city that was, at the time, a significant rival to Florence.
Neptune	In Roman mythology: the god of the sea and Jupiter's brother.
Palazzo Vecchio	Magnificent Florentine palace built from 1299 and now used as the city's town hall.
Pegasus	In Greek mythology: a winged horse. Zeus turned Pegasus into a constellation as a reward for his loyal service.
Peloponnese	Geographically, the southern section of Greece.
Phaethon	In Greek mythology: Phaethon asked his father Helios if he could drive the sun chariot for one day. He did so but fell from the sky and was killed.
Pisa	An Italian city, west of Florence.

Platonic Academy Founded by the Medicis in 1438 and dedicated to the study of traditional Western philosophers, such as Plato and Socrates.

Ponte di Rubaconte An arched bridge over the Arno River that was, during this period, the longest bridge in Florence. It is now known as Ponte alle Grazie, having been rebuilt in 1945 after the original was destroyed.

Purgatorio The setting for Part 2 of Dante Alighieri's epic poem, *The Divine Comedy.* A popular text of the time, the poem was completed in 1320.

Salacia In Roman mythology: a female companion to the god, Neptune. She represented the power and potential disorder of water in nature.

San Romano A town outside Florence. In 1432, the city-states of Florence and Sienna fought a battle there, which both cities claimed to have won.

Scutari A town, now a city, in Albania. The town was controlled by the Republic of Venice until Ottoman (Turkish) forces invaded in the mid-1470s.

Socrates 470–399 BC. Greek philosopher whose famous question-answer model of inquiry is known as the Socratic method.

Tartary At this time, Europeans referred to Asia as Tartary without knowing full details of the continent's geography.

Venice City in the north-east corner of Italy which is built on water. Its location made it favourable for those who wished to trade to the East.

Acknowledgements

The definition of *sfumato* that is used, in summary, by the master in the Epilogue is derived from *The Story of Art* (pocket edition) by E.H. Gombrich, Phaidon Press, London, 2006.

Annalisa's Prayer of Consolation (Chapter 7: Repentance) comes from *Prayers of the Middle Ages: Light from a Thousand Years*, edited by James Manning Potts, Nashville, 1954; Project Gutenberg, 2015, https://www.gutenberg.org/files/48242/48242-h/48242-h.htm#c9, accessed 11 July 2020.

Some words and phrases in Annalisa's description of her angry father (Chapter 21: Ecstasy) come from Virgil's description of Charon in *Aeneid Book 6*, lines 298 – 301, translated by J. W. Mackail, 2007; Project Gutenberg, https://www.gutenberg.org/files/22456/22456-h/22456-h.htm#BOOK_SIXTH, accessed 18 August 2020.

The quote about Francesco Melzi in the Author's Note comes from Giorgio Vasari, *Lives of the Most Eminent Painters and Sculptors* (Volume 4, page 99), translated by Gaston Du C. de Vere, London, 1913;

Project Gutenberg, 2009, https://www.gutenberg.org/cache/epub/28420/pg28420-images.html#Page_99, accessed 12 October 2020.

The biography referenced in the Author's Note is *Leonardo da Vinci* by Walter Isaacson, Simon and Schuster, New York, 2018.

About the Author

Richard Yaxley is a Brisbane-based author. His novels include *Joyous and Moonbeam* (Scholastic 2013) and *This Is My Song* (winner of the 2018 Prime Minister's Literary Award for Young Adult Literature; winner of the 2019 ACU Book of the Year Award; finalist in the 2017 Queensland Literary Awards). *The Happiness Quest* was published by Scholastic in 2018 and listed as a 2019 CBCA Notable for Older Readers. More recent novels include *A New Kind Of Everything* (Scholastic 2020) and *Harmony* (Scholastic 2021), which was longlisted for the Children's and Young Adult section of the ARA Historical Novel Prize.

Richard is also a past winner of the Queensland Premier's Literary Award (*Drink the Air,* 2010), the Walter Stone Life-writing Award (2016), a Fellowship from the May Gibbs Literature Trust (2016) and, in 2022, the inaugural QWC-Varuna Fellowship for Established Writers. He is a regular presenter of writing workshops, an ambassador for Australia Reads, and was a judge for the Prime Minister's Literary Awards in 2021.

Richard has two Masters Degrees, in Cultural Studies and Human Rights, and has written or co-written over twenty-five textbooks for classrooms across Australia, as well as plays and poetry. In 2011, he was awarded a Medal in the Order of Australia (OAM).

For further information, go to:
https://richardwyaxley.com